CLUES TO THE EXCITEMENT ABOUT NINE-TIME EDGAR AWARD NOMINEE ROBERT BARNARD

"The wryest wit and most scathing satire in today's mystery."—*Chicago Sun-Times*

"Barnard [has] an eye for the self-delusion and hypocrisy in all of us . . . and the result is a growing series of mysteries that are entertaining . . . quite funny . . . and acutely observing."—*The Boston Globe*

"There's no one quite like Robert Barnard in his ability to combine chills and chuckles and then sprinkle the whole with delicious irony."—*San Diego Union*

"Robert Barnard remains one of the wittiest of the mysterians."—*Los Angeles Times Book Review*

"Few writers are better equipped to handle the intricate plotting and larger-than-life characters."—*Denver Post*

"Robert Barnard['s] wit and invention have enlivened many a murder investigation."
—*The Washington Post Book World*

A CITY of STRANGERS

Dell Books by Robert Barnard

A
City of
STRANGERS

◆

ROBERT BARNARD

◆

A Dell Book

Published by
Dell Publishing
a division of
Bantam Doubleday Dell Publishing Group, Inc.
666 Fifth Avenue
New York, New York 10103

ISBN: 0-440-20750-9

Reprinted by arrangement with Charles Scribner's Sons,
Macmillan Publishing Company, New York, New York

Printed in the United States of America

Published simultaneously in Canada

September 1991

10 9 8 7 6 5 4 3 2 1

RAD

Unable to define anything I can hardly speak,
and still I love the place for what I wanted it to be
as much as for what it unashamedly is
now for me, a city of strangers, alien and bleak.

Dannie Abse, *"Return to Cardiff"*

A CITY of STRANGERS

Chapter ONE

*I*t had been quite an ordinary day up until then.

Except that Carol Southgate, in her first term as a teacher, did not have as yet ordinary days: There was about all of them an element of challenge, fear, discovery. Then at ten-thirty she scanned casually the list of children in Burtle Middle School's 3B—her own class—and said "Michael Phelan." She was not entirely familiar with the names and was looking for a child who had not yet read for her; otherwise she would have remembered about the Phelans.

A boy, smallish for his twelve years, looked up at her momentarily from a desk toward the back of the class. Then he looked down at his book and began.

He read hesitantly at first, in a strong Yorkshire accent, but he swiftly gained confidence, so that by the second verse the reading had swing, panache, drama:

Rats!
They fought the dogs and killed the cats,
And bit the babies in the cradles,
And ate the cheese out of the vats,
And licked the soup from the cooks' own ladles . . .

The poetry books that 3B were using were old and not really suitable. It sometimes seemed as if teachers and pupils were supposed to be grateful that they had any books at all. Carol sat back, suffused by a rare feeling of well-being, of positive pleasure. This, surely, was the miracle that happened now and again in all teachers' careers— the life-enriching miracle that made the drudgery worthwhile. And this boy was one of the Phelans, of whom she had heard so much. She let Michael read for four verses, his voice increasing all the time in relish and sense of occasion. Then she said, as calmly as she could:

"That was very nice. Wayne Fothergill—can you get the swing of it as Michael has?"

Wayne Fothergill, of course, couldn't. The reading declined into hesitancy and dullness. A cloud, as so often outside, came over the sun.

Nevertheless there had been this momentary brightening up of Carol's morning, and it buoyed her up. Moments of surprise and joy had been few in her teaching career thus far. At coffee break she said to her new and as yet half-known colleagues:

"You've given me the wrong idea about the Phelans. Michael read quite beautifully this morning."

They turned on her in scorn, Dot Fenton being the one who led the attack.

"Oh, *Michael*! If you've only known Michael you haven't experienced the Phelans. If you'd had Kevin, now—he was *vicious*. Or that little slut June. Or Cilla. And there's a horrible little girl called Jackie who's just started Junior and who's *really* going to present problems when she comes here. Oh dear! To imagine that you know the Phelans when you only know Michael!"

"Michael is all right," said Bob McEvoy quietly.

Registering his comment, as she had for the past month registered him, Carol sat with him at lunch break. They both ate sandwiches wrapped in grease-proof paper and drank from thermoses prepared at home. Carol had been anxious to avoid any suggestion of favoritism, but during History with 3B after coffee break she had asked Michael to read a passage about the death of Wolsey. He had read that beautifully too.

"Is it true what they say about the Phelans?" she now asked Bob. He nodded.

"Pretty much. Kevin was indescribably nasty. The sort of boy you have to physically restrain yourself from beating up—to knock quietness into him, if not sense. He left two or three years ago. I was a young teacher then, new and uncertain, and it was touch and go, I can tell you."

"Whether you . . . laid hands on him or not?"

"Yes. And don't be shocked. You'll know the feeling, I can tell you."

"What about the others?"

"I only know June, who's left, and Cilla, who's here at the moment. They're pretty dreadful, yes."

"You're interested in drama, aren't you?"

Everyone knew that about Bob McEvoy. Officially he was the P.E. teacher, with bits of other things thrown in—Religious Instruction and Mathematics with the lower grades. But he had acted with the Youth Theatre in his time, and performance was in his blood. He grinned and said:

"Would you like me to hear your Michael Phelan read?"

"He's not *mine*. . . . Well, yes. Are you putting anything on this year?"

"Oh, yes. There's the school play in February, but also the big production—kids from all the schools in Sleate—coming off in May, in the Civic Theatre. It's *Saint Joan* this year."

"Michael for page," said Carol promptly.

"There's also Speech Day in November. I'm getting together a few kids to do things—read poems, perform tiny playlets. If he's as good as you say, if he's really got a sense of rhythm, maybe he could do a poem or two."

"Am I hearing things?" It was Dot Fenton, who had given the bitter little diatribe on the Phelans at break. "Are we talking about a *Phelan* performing at *Speech* Day?"

"Why not?" said Carol, suddenly prickly.

"Can't you imagine what he would *look* like? They're all filthy, and June positively smells—I don't like to think what of. You must be out of your minds."

"His mother could make a bit of effort."

"My dear young thing, don't talk about what she could do, talk about what she would do. His mother doesn't know the meaning of the word effort."

"I've never seen Michael worse than grubby, and what child isn't that sometimes? Anyway, why should the kids who get up at Speech Day always be the ones with the neat trousers and socks and the nice clean shirts?"

"Because we try to maintain standards, that's why," snapped Dot dismissively, and went on her way. Carol, regaining her cool, raised her eyebrows at Bob.

"I'll hear him read," Bob said quietly.

It was Friday of that same week that, walking home together after school, Carol and Bob McEvoy saw Michael Phelan ahead of them on the road up the hill.

Burtle, the suburb of Sleate which the school served and where they lived, was not one of the most attractive parts of Yorkshire. It had not been made so by nature, and the actions of the Council in demolishing much of its nineteenth-century heritage had not improved matters. Semidetacheds and council housing estates alternated with the occasional high-rise block, but sometimes, in gaps between the red-brick gables and the concrete slabs, one caught glimpses of Victorian Camelots or mill-owners' Georgian. It had, Carol had decided, a certain raggedy vigor, sorely frayed in that era of mass un-employment.

Michael and his friend were larking around, pushing and chasing each other along and across the pavement, never venturing into the traffic. They watched them, two very normal children.

"He read very well," said Bob.

"I knew he would."

"Whether he can act at all I didn't find out, but speaking is half the battle, as a rule. He could certainly do something at Speech Day."

Ahead of them Michael's friend branched off to go home, while he himself trudged solidly up the hill toward his own home.

"Why don't you tell him now?" asked Carol, and they speeded up their walk.

When they came up behind him he turned and grinned at them, noting the fact that they were together and probably filing it for lascivious comment to a friend in the morning, in the way schoolboys have.

"You read for me very nicely this morning, Michael," Bob said. "I thought it might be an idea if you recited something for the parents at Speech Day."

The boy's forehead creased.

"I don't know about that. . . . I don't know what my Dad would say. . . . He's a bit . . . Well, we don't go in for that sort of thing in our family."

"But there's no reason why he should object, surely, is there?"

"You don't know my Dad." Michael Phelan grinned. He seemed to have a certain pride in his dad, as a well-known character. "I shouldn't think I'd be going to school at all, if he had his way."

"Oh, come on, Michael: Everyone has to go to school."

Michael Phelan twisted his face and threw his voice into that of a hectoring, opinionated adult.

" 'Bloody waste of time. No bloody use at all. Should be out earning a living.' That's what my Dad says. I heard Mrs. Makepeace say my Dad has opinions on everything, and all of them are wrong."

"Who's Mrs. Makepeace?"

"Our next-door neighbor. She helps a bit—with my clothes and that. . . . Maybe I'll talk to her about Speech Day. Sometimes my Dad listens to her."

"You do that, Michael."

"Would it mean dressing posh? I know just what my Dad would say if it did. Specially if it meant buying new clothes for me."

"I'm sure if you could get Mrs. Makepeace to help a little you would look fine."

They had reached the top of the hill, and they turned off

into the council estate where Michael lived. By now Bob McEvoy was off his route home, but his curiosity was roused. Carol was walking quietly behind them thinking that, given time, Bob could bring out unguessed-at qualities in this odd, charming boy.

The Belfield Grove Estate was built as rented accommodation by the Sleate City Council shortly after the war, and the houses, though uniform and possessing few graces, had at least escaped the brutal impersonality of later council architecture. Now it was run-down, with slates off roofs and paint peeling from the window frames. Some of the gardens were beautifully cared for, while others had run wild for years, and still others were the dumping-ground for abandoned motorcycles and cars, disused rabbit hutches or pigeon lofts. Along the road as they walked, chocolate wrappings fluttered around their feet, and in the gutters lay odd tin cans and take-away pizza cartons. The inhabitants of the Estate did not have the middle-class habit of getting on the phone if the street cleaners had not been around recently, so for the most part the Council forgot the Estate existed. Some of the houses had been sold at knock-down prices to their tenants, and some of them had done odd things to the outsides—painted over the brickwork, or had a new frontage attached of simulated stone that looked nothing like stone. Sharp-eyed dogs roamed around, looking for succulent leftovers in tins or a friendly child with a sweet.

Michael was by now chattering happily on.

"I liked that poem I read for you the other day, Miss. That one about the rats. P'raps I could read that at Speech Day."

"It's a little bit long," said Bob. "Perhaps we could try

something from *Old Possum's Book of Practical Cats*. A lot of people have seen *Cats,* or know the music."

"Did he write a book about dogs too?" Michael asked innocently. "I like dogs better. I'd like to have a dog and—"

"Mike, you stupid git! How often do I have to tell you not to talk to strange men?"

The voice, recognizably that of Michael's imitation, came from the other side of the hedge. They stopped by the gate.

"It's all right, Dad," said Michael. "He's a teacher."

"What difference does that make? There's pooftah teachers, aren't there?"

"Don't worry. That's just my Dad," whispered Michael.

They stood for a moment, looking at each other. He was a heavily built man, of under middle height, now into his forties and gone badly to seed. Though the day was not warm he was wearing a vest that displayed brawny and tattooed arms gone nastily to flesh, and a prominent beer gut. His trousers were filthy, and he sat on a crate in a garden littered with the dismembered remains of cars, a can of beer at his side, looking up at them with a derisive, gap-toothed smile. It was the smile that told Carol that he had known that Michael was talking to teachers, that it was that had made him call out.

"I'm just going in to Mrs. Makepeace's, Dad," Michael said.

"I don't give a bugger where you go," said Mr. Phelan.

It was said with the same derisive smile through deplorable, blackened teeth. It was a challenge, a metaphorical thumbing of the nose. It said: I don't give a damn about teachers. They don't impress me. I don't change my behavior for them. I don't give a damn about anybody. My whole life is a rude noise made in the face of the world.

Bob and Carol made no gesture of greeting. It would have been jeeringly flung back at them. As Michael ran into the house next door they walked quietly on.

"The miracles of heredity," said Carol.

"What are you thinking—that someone slipped in quickly while Jack there was out at the pub? That Mary Phelan had it off with a smooth-talking newsreader for Yorkshire Television? You wouldn't think so if you'd seen Mary, I assure you."

Carol giggled.

"No, I just meant that funny things happen in families. I mean, look at good, conscientious, upright George III and his queen producing that long succession of appalling boys. It must happen the other way round sometimes. . . . What are you coming this way for, anyway?"

"I'm not turning back to have my masculinity impugned again by that jerk. Anyway, I wanted to see where you live."

"Well, you'll soon see. We're coming to it now."

The road was sloping down, and on their right was the last of the Belfield Grove houses. The narrow road that went from left to right of the Estate was Wynton Lane, and it consisted of a row of six near-identical houses, one of them currently up for sale. They were substantial late-Victorian residences, built of stone, with steps down to basement flats. The front gardens contained late roses, hydrangea and berberis bushes, and laburnums and flowering cherries in the process of losing their leaves. Behind them were further gardens, a lane with garages, and beyond that school playing fields stretching out to where the main road curved. The houses seemed confident, assertive, yet isolated.

"I live in the basement of the nearest one," said Carol. "It's Daphne Bridewell's house. She's an ex-deputy head-mistress at Burtle Middle School. She's a bit odd, but awfully sweet."

Bob McEvoy was quiet, and she looked up at him.

"They're rather splendid houses, aren't they?"

"Yes. Very fine. But so isolated . . . so exposed. . . . Somehow they have a smell of fear."

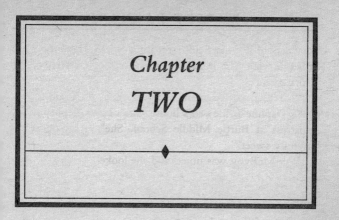

Chapter
TWO

———————————◆———————————

Morning broke, or rather crumbled slowly, over Willow Bank, over Ashdene, The Laburnums, Rosetree Cottage, York House, and The Hollies, the houses that together made up Wynton Lane. Looking out at the light fog, thick with incipient drizzle and the threat of autumn, the inhabitants ate their chosen forms of breakfast before taking up a new day in their lives.

————◆————

Adrian Eastlake stood at the window of Willow Bank, plate in hand, eating the last of his toast and marmalade. His toast was always cold after he had taken up the tray with the soft-boiled or scrambled eggs to his mother. But over the years Adrian had come to like it that way.

He looked out from the dining-room window over to the Belfield Grove Estate.

It was his day for working at the Burtle Social Security Office, checking up on their files and administrative procedures. It was long ago that they had stopped sending him out on casework. Blessed, blessed relief. He disliked his days at the Burtle office, though, because his shortest way there was through the Estate. Past the Phelans'.

It was foolish, of course, a weakness in him. The day when he had visited the Phelans after complaints about child neglect and had been comprehensively routed by that dreadful man was years ago now, and should have been forgotten. Only it had not been, either by him or by Jack Phelan. If he was sitting on his step, standing in his doorway with a can of beer, or tinkering with an ancient car on the road outside, the occasion would be memorialized in a jeering epithet, or a rude question. "Snooper," "mole," even "workhouse master" had been flung at him at various times, and the fact that he had the sympathy of all the Phelans' neighbors did little to salve the wound, for Adrian was a man who desperately hated public embarrassment. The man was known to be a barbarian, but somehow that didn't make his barbarities easier to bear.

And there was something else, something the neighbors could know nothing about. This was the idea that had come to him in the aftermath of his routing. The idea that this was the man who . . . that this was the man who had . . . that Jack Phelan was responsible for his mother's condition.

At the thought of his mother Adrian Eastlake experienced that sudden contraction of the heart, that pain, that was so familiar to him. A memory of her as she had been, in all her fragile beauty, flooded through him. Thus had she been as he had grown from boyhood into his teens, twenty years ago, shouldering alone the burdens of parenthood, putting a brave front on genteel poverty. He saw her as some infinitely fine, delicate piece of china, waiting to be smashed by—by Jack Phelan?

There was no evidence, of course. How could there be evidence, let alone charges, when she had refused to let him go to the police, refused even to talk about it after that first, frantic sobbing out of broken phrases? And though Jack Phelan had been in trouble with the police times without number, it had never been for . . . that sort of thing. And yet when Adrian thought about his brutality, his blatancy, his goatish gloating, the conviction that it was he, could only have been he, took hold of his heart in an iron grip. He knew his neighbors, knew the people on the Estate: They were decent, ordinary people. Only Phelan, chronically unemployed, hovering round the area like a malevolent, derisive shadow, would have been *there* that afternoon, in the vicinity. Only he would have been capable of—would rejoice in—smashing a thing of delicate beauty.

He turned aside from the gray prospect outside the window and took his plate and cup to the kitchen. Then he went upstairs. He knocked as always at her door. She looked up as he entered, and smiled with that recollection of her wonderful beauty that lines and sunken cheeks could not entirely erase. She was wearing her pink day robe—she loved gentle colors—and was surrounded by the morning papers.

"Are you off, dear?"

"In a minute or two. Will you be all right, darling?"

"Of course. I have the Angela Thirkell—I'm so happy to be reading it again. And I have my scrapbook. There's such a lovely picture of the Princess of Wales at Dr. Barnardo's—and such a wonderful speech she gave. I think I'll paste that in too."

Rosamund Eastlake always referred to her as "the Princess of Wales," or, in writing (she wrote quite often to newspapers about the royal family) as "Diana, Princess of Wales." The solecism "Princess Diana" never passed her lips, and "Princess Di" made her shudder. The fact that she took newspapers that habitually used that form and frequently spoke of the royals in tones that were hectoring, lip-licking, or covertly contemptuous was attributable to the fact that they so often had awfully good pictures to compensate for the distress that the letterpress brought. Her scrapbooks filled two bookcases in her room, and had overflowed into the little spare bedroom. They were the source of much of the pleasure she got from life these days.

"Is it your day for Burtle, Adrian?"

"Yes, it is."

"I forget the days. . . . Don't go through the Estate. You get so tensed up whenever you do that. Go up to the main road and round."

"All right, I will, my darling."

"I do so hate to see you worried. You are so good to me—I depend so much on you. What would you like for dinner?"

"Whatever you fancy, darling."

"Would you like lamb chops?"

"That would be lovely."

"Pick some up at Dewbury's, then. You say he remembers me, the man there. Not many do, these days. Don't work too hard, Adrian. They're not worth it. I'll see you this evening."

Rosamund Eastlake raised her cheek, and Adrian bent to kiss her goodbye. He went downstairs, checked that the back door was locked and bolted, and let himself out of the front, locking it carefully behind him. Then he went down the front path, past roses sad from the rain, and out into Wynton Lane. He turned right and continued up the main road, the route that would allow him to skirt the Belfield Grove Estate.

◆

"There goes Adrian Eastlake," said Lynn Packard, his voice edged with contempt as he too stood at the window, looking out from York House, coffee cup in hand. His wife and sons sat finishing the remains of a hearty breakfast, but Lynn was a quick eater. "Look at him: Up to the main road because he can't face the Estate, as usual."

"When did you last walk through the Estate?" asked his wife Jennifer. Lynn was not listening.

"That man has a personality problem. He hasn't got one."

"Poor Adrian. Just because he can't face going through the Estate."

"He's the archetypal wimp. That woman has him just where she wants him. The funny thing is, that's where *he* wants to be too." His mouth curled. "A quarter of a mile extra walking because he won't go through Belfield Grove."

"You could do with a bit more exercise yourself," said his wife. But she knew that Lynn was off on a track of his own and not listening.

"A quarter of a mile, because he can't face up to the Phelans," he repeated.

"The Phelans are going up in the world," said his wife,

19

in a special, distinct voice that she used when she wanted to get through to him. "Gareth says one of the boys is going to recite something at Speech Day."

"What?" Sure enough, this time Lynn Packard heard. He wheeled round on his wife and two sons. *"What?"*

"Michael Phelan is going to read a poem at Speech Day," said Gareth, shrugging.

"He's all right, is Michael," said Tristram. "He's not like the others."

"Oh, my God!" said Lynn, and Jennifer could see he was working up to one of his petty scenes. "We send our kids to State schools and what do we get? Tristram says 'He's all right, is Michael,' like some Yorkshire yob. And some smelly kid from the council estate gets to take the star role at Speech Day. I tell you, Jennifer, this is political. Some smart-arse left-winger on the teaching staff is trying to score a point. Who's arranging this, eh?"

"Mr. McEvoy," said Gareth. "He does all that sort of thing. I did read for him and he said it was quite nice, but it didn't have quite enough life."

Lynn was not listening again. He swung round on his wife.

"I've said it before and I'll say it again: The time is coming when we'll have no choice. We'll have to send the pair of them to a private school."

"You'd have done it long ago," his wife pointed out, "if we could have afforded it."

And that was the rub. Lynn had many of the characteristics of a yuppie: He dressed like one, he spoke like one (his voice high, somewhere between the hectoring and the hysterical, the vowels twisted by some invisible vocal screw), he played squash and computer games, and got boisterous or objectionable in nightclubs and casinos. But when it came down to it he was not quite young enough or, crucially, quite upwardly mobile enough to be a yuppie. He was manager of the Foodwise supermarket in town— young to be a manager, quite well paid, and yet . . . not quite well paid enough. Not to send two boys to a private school.

They had discussed it often in the last few years, and Jennifer had always detailed the changes in their life-style that the cost of a private education for the boys would entail: the smaller car, the end of holidays abroad, of those lavish restaurant meals that were adding to Lynn's waistline, of the smart clothes, renewed every year. In the end Lynn saw sense: He was devoted to his life-style.

Jennifer too, in her way. She had been an excellent wife for him, on his way up. She had entertained successfully— learned the right cutlery for each course and how to set it out, the right wine for each dish, learned that when the managing director of the Foodwise chain came to dinner one praised Foodwise frozen meals, though one did not serve them.

A change had come over Lynn in recent years, though. Previously he had been aggressively out for himself. Now that had widened, had become an article of faith: Self-interest was the guiding principle of life, the market was supreme, and people who disregarded that fact were here-tics, or just plain ignorant. He had become a born-again free marketeer. The thrusting young man she had found exciting; the strident evangelist, she had to admit, was something of a bore.

"We've been into all that," she said, trying to conceal

the weariness in her voice. Lynn stood there fuming, as he always did when he couldn't get what he wanted.

"We could move," he said. "Look at what Pickering is asking for The Hollies. Ninety-five thousand. These houses are going up-market."

"Maybe—but that didn't stop Pickering moving away," Jennifer pointed out. "Anyway, where would we move *to*? I must say I don't see you moving anywhere further *down*-market."

"A cottage out of town . . ."

"Cottages cost the earth. And then you'd have the expense of the extra petrol."

Lynn stood there, his incipient second chin bobbing in irritation. He turned to the boys.

"Come on. Get your things on. I haven't got all day." He looked at his wife as he began bustling the pair of them out to the car. "We're stuck," he said bitterly. "Stuck somewhere between the filthy rich and the filthy poor."

It was one of Lynn's jokes, always brought out defensively when people came to dinner who would know that Burtle was not a socially acceptable part of Sleate. Jennifer smiled. She knew it was beyond a wife's power to change her husband's little jokes. As the three males raced to the car she began clearing away the breakfast things.

◆

"You should eat wholemeal," said Evie Soames, looking up from the paper on which her breakfast plate was perched. "You've no idea what that muck contains."

"I don't *like* wholemeal," said Steven Copperwhite. "Particularly for toast."

He pressed down the toaster containing the slice of white, prepacked sliced loaf and looked around for the marmalade.

The kitchen of Ashdene was a mess as usual. The washing-up from the night before had not been done, and Evie's special dishes always seemed to involve so many pots and pans, not to mention the fact that the grill was thick with grease from his own pork chops. The kitchen table was littered with newspapers, *New Statesman*s, *Spare Rib*s, photocopies from books, and books from the university library that Evie was using for her thesis, *Toward a Feminist Linguistics*. Evie was eating muesli. He wished she would eat something else at breakfast time, something that was less obviously a fashionable joke.

He poked around the table, looking for the marmalade. Evie absently plunged her hand into the clutter and produced it.

"Your trouble," she said, "is you're not programmed for mess."

That was true. If Evie lived alone here, or alone with the occasional man for the night, she would live with the mess quite happily, and perhaps make a vigorous foray against it once a month. But he was not happy with mess, which was why it usually fell to him to clear it up. That was quite fair, and he acknowledged it: If it bothered him, it was up to him to do something about it. Evie had made it quite clear when they had taken up together that she had no interest in housework, nor any conscience about it. She had been admirably honest altogether. She was wonderful fun in bed, an excellent cook of a rather special kind of food he disliked, and an appalling housekeeper. It was working out, the two of them, working out fine, but there were times when he longed back to the ordered routines of his marriage, the peace and security of it, as the Magi longed back to their summer palaces.

A smell of burning pervaded the kitchen for some seconds before the toast popped up.

"You have to readjust it for white," said Evie. "No gumption in it."

Steven scraped, and buttered, and spread marmalade.

"What are you doing today?" Evie asked.

"I thought I'd stay home and work on the book. The students are demonstrating against the plan for student loans, and all the lectures and tutorials are cancelled for the day."

"I know that, dumbcluck. I *am* a student. Aren't you going to support them?"

"Of course, I support them. It'll be an appallingly retrograde step. We'll soon find ourselves saddled with the American system, with students working half the night in fast-food joints or petrol stations to put themselves through university."

"I didn't ask whether you supported them. I asked whether you were going *along* to support them."

"Oh well . . . I may well go along later. But the opportunity to do some quiet work at home for once seemed too good to miss. What are you doing?"

Evie registered the change of subject but began collecting her things together for the day.

"I've got a PND support group after work. Then I may go along to the youth club tonight. There's a nasty bunch of National Front boys trying to infiltrate it. That horrible thug Kevin Phelan, among others."

Steven's mind registered that PND meant Post-Natal Depression. He knew all Evie's acronyms. He also knew better than to ask why Evie went to a post-natal depression group when she had never given birth. He knew that the point was the support rather than the parturition. It was really very good of Evie to go along to the youth club, because as a rule youth clubs weren't her thing at all. In fact, Evie was altogether good.

"I don't like the thought of you tangling with a tough like Kevin Phelan."

"Oh, I'm more than a match for *him*," said Evie breezily, slinging her bag onto her shoulder and waving goodbye.

Steven ran some washing-up water and piled plates in the sink. Then he went through to his study. His desk was piled high with novels, with the manuscript of the first two chapters of his book placed neatly in the middle in front of the chair. His current project was a study of old age in the modern British novel, with special reference to works by Muriel Spark, Elizabeth Taylor, Paul Bailey, Kingsley Amis, and others. He hoped that this would be the book that would finally assure him of an associate professorship before it was too late. He would have felt more confident if his previous book, *The Burden of Male Dominance* (studies in *Dombey, Middlemarch, The Mayor of Casterbridge,* etc.) had not still been making the rounds of the academic publishers.

He could never settle down to work immediately. He had to walk around the room, get his future day into some sort of shape in his mind first. It would have been easier if he had still smoked, but Evie was very hot on the subject of smoking. He touched books, took up the *Times Literary Supplement* and looked at the crossword, then peered at one of his most prized possessions, the photograph of Balliol College in 1957, with himself standing in the sixth row. Then he walked restlessly over to the window to look out toward the Belfield Grove Estate. He remembered Evie's mother, on her one visit, looking over to the close-packed houses and saying in her horrible upper-class drawl: "What ghastly little rabbit hutches! They must be able to hear each other at the lavatory." She had left quickly, after the row she had come intending to have, and before she had had the chance to test their own sanitary arrangements.

He felt a sudden twinge of uneasiness at the thought of Evie confronting that vicious young thug Kevin Phelan. Then he wondered if it was uneasiness he felt. Certainly he felt it would have been easier if he could simply have volunteered to go along to protect her, or at any rate to make sure she was all right. But of course he knew Evie would reject that idea with a derisive laugh.

He went back to the kitchen, cleaned the plates and put them to drain, then piled up all the saucepans and the frying pan in the water. Then he sat down at his desk in front of the manuscript that in his own mind he was beginning to call *You're Only Young Twice*. Old age was a depressing subject. He himself, though not old, was beginning to feel his age. Fifty-two to Evie's twenty-six. If it had been the other way round, people would have made ribald jokes, talked about "toy-boys." Even as it was he knew that people talked. . . .

There came upon him a niggling sense that his life had somehow become out of joint, that the shape and fitness it had once had were now gone, leaving muddle, frustration.

He got up from his desk. Perhaps he would go along to that demonstration after all.

Algy Cartwright, in Rosetree Cottage, cleared away the remainder of his breakfast and ran some water in the kitchen sink. The scrambled eggs hadn't been perfect, but they had been better than they had been when he first had tried to cook them. He watched the sports news on breakfast television, then went backward and forward between the washing-up and the television. His washing-up was better than it had been too. In fact everything was better except the terrible gaping hole in his life left by the death of his wife. He looked out of the kitchen window. A drizzle seemed to be starting, and darkness hung in the air. What did the day ahead hold for him? He knew the answer to that. Nothing.

After the nine o'clock news there would be a witless phone-in on television called *Open Air*. He always prayed he would have the strength to turn programs like that off—to settle down to reading, gardening, even housework. Today, with the drizzle outside and the murk inside, he knew he would not have the strength. There was nothing to be done in the garden, and reading had never meant much to him, apart from the daily paper. He was a man whose life had always centered round people, and now he was retired, and widowed.

On days like this he longed for death.

---◆---

In The Laburnums Daphne Bridewell had called down the stairs and asked Carol Southgate up for a proper breakfast. As a former teacher and deputy-headmistress herself she had strong opinions on starting the day in a demanding job on no more than a piece of toast or a plate of cereal.

Daphne Bridewell had strong opinions on most things, in fact.

Carol enjoyed the poached eggs and bacon and mushrooms for a change, and enjoyed talking to Daphne. Though her basement flat was self-contained there were few days when they did not exchange the odd word, and many when they had long, absorbing conversations. Daphne knew all about her interest in Michael Phelan, and was sensible and experienced enough to treat it for what it was—not the "discovery" of a potential genius, merely concern for a talented and attractive child.

"How are things going with Michael?" she asked.

"Oh, fine. He's going to do a piece from *Old Possum* for Speech Day. All the other kids seem pleased—they like him. Of course, there has been comment in the staff room."

Daphne Bridewell raised her eyebrows.

"Why 'of course'? Who commented?"

"Dot Fenton."

"Oh, yes," said Daphne in a neutral voice. She had an ex-teacher's care about how much she said. "She was there in my time."

"I fail to see, personally, how keeping down an intelligent child because he's not well-scrubbed can be construed as keeping up standards," said Carol waspishly.

"It's an odd notion for a teacher, certainly. I'm sure he'll do very well, and everyone will see he's a child to be brought on. . . . You're worried about him, though, aren't you, dear?"

"Yes. Yes, of course I am. When you think of the examples he's surrounded by: those parents, that horrible elder brother, the sister who's apparently sleeping round at sixteen. . . ."

"He's got through life this far, apparently, without taking harm."

"But adolescence is coming up. Think of the pressures."

Daphne looked at her closely.

"You want to do something about him, don't you?"

Carol nodded vigorously.

"Oh, yes. But what is there *to* do?"

"You could speak to the neighbor."

"I thought about that. But what excuse could I make?"

"I don't think, since the parents are so appalling, that you would need an excuse. She would quite understand. Just choose your time when you visit her. You wouldn't want Jack Phelan to know what you were doing. Maybe she has a phone and you could arrange it in advance." She took Carol's hand over the table. "There's no reason why you shouldn't do something, my dear. There's every reason why a teacher should feel a special interest in some pupils. But do it quietly. Otherwise you could do him harm."

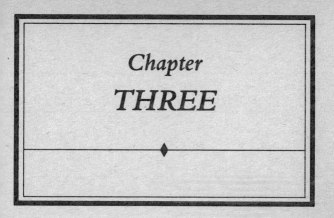

Chapter

THREE

Mrs. Makepeace, Michael's anchor to normality, indeed had a phone. In a free period at school next morning Carol leafed through the dog-eared telephone directory in the staff common room and found Makepeace, L., 37 Belfield Grove Avenue. That would be her. It was quiet in the common room so Carol rang her there and then, struggling with feelings of diffidence and a sense that she was straying into unauthorized territory. The voice at the other end of the line was elderly, slightly wary, yet sympathetic. When Carol had explained that she was Michael's teacher and that she would like to come round and talk about him, it was obvious that Mrs. Makepeace was surprised.

"About Michael? I don't know . . ."

"You see, he's rather a bright boy—"

"He is that."

"And, as you must know, his parents—"

"Oh, you'll do no good talking to *them*."

"No. But I do feel I need to talk to someone. I hear so much about the other Phelan children, and it would be terrible if Michael went the same way. If we two could just have a chat . . ."

There was a pause at the other end. Carol suspected that Mrs. Makepeace was reluctant to get on the wrong side of her neighbors, and this was confirmed by her next words.

"Do you think you could come after dark? You see my own are long past school age, and if he knows you're Michael's teacher, and coming to see me . . . well, the long and the short of it is, he could turn nasty. He's very quick to turn nasty, is Jack Phelan, as you may have heard, and if I'm to get anywhere with him I have to keep on the right side of him."

"Of course, I quite understand that. I live just near. Shall we say half past eight tonight?"

"Happen he'll be in t'pub by then anyway," said Lottie Makepeace. "I'll brew a pot of tea and we can have a talk."

Carol was telling Bob McEvoy all this at coffee break, as they sat companionably in two corner armchairs, when Dot Fenton breezed up.

"I've been reading about kids like your Michael Phelan," she said, breaking without apology into their conversation.

"He's not *mine*."

"There's an article in *The Teacher* about kids with hopeless family backgrounds. All the kids turn out as you'd expect, except occasionally the one who comes through it all unscathed and becomes happy and successful. There's a report on it—American, I think—and a book called *The Invulnerable Child*."

"I'd like to see the article," said Carol, willing to go half-way to meet Dot Fenton's change in tone.

"*Any*way, they say what happens is, the child subconsciously discards the parents and the home and latches on to someone—a relative, or neighbor, or something—who *is* normal and stable and provides him with what he needs."

"Mrs. Makepeace!" said Carol triumphantly.

"Who?"

"Michael's next-door neighbor. Apparently he's very fond of her and is always in there."

"There you are, you see," said Dot, with a nod of self-satisfaction. "That's how it was done."

Carol resented Dot's talking of Michael as if he were some kind of conjuring trick."

"That's all very well," she muttered to Bob, "but I don't see how a child *can* be invulnerable, do you?"

"Oh, Steven, I forgot to tell you," said Evie, standing in the door of his study, her bag of books slung over her shoulder. "The girls will be coming tonight."

"If *I'd* called them girls . . ." said Steven. "Does that mean you just want me to make myself scarce, or do I have to go out?"

"Well, Val and Marian never *really* talk freely if they know there's a man in the house."

"Sensitive friends you have."

"Pig."

Steven Copperwhite looked at her as she turned to go. She had been hunched over a pile of Scandinavian linguistics theses at breakfast and he hadn't seen her face.

"What's that on your forehead?"

"Oh, nothing," said Evie, shrugging.

"It's a scar."

"OK, it's a scar. I had a bit of an argie-bargie with the Phelan boy last night."

"You didn't tell me when you came to bed."

"You didn't ask. Look, stop fussing, Steven, right? You're imagining this boy as a big, strong thug. Forget it: He's got spindle shanks, biceps like peanuts, and his Union Jack tee-shirt flaps on his skinny chest."

"But everyone says he's a vicious little horror."

"Oh, he is that. But I can handle *his* like."

"It doesn't look like it."

"Oh, *he* went slinking away, I can tell you," said Evie gaily. "Look, Steven: Forget the protective chivalry bit, eh? It doesn't suit you at all."

She smiled, waved, and shut the door. From the study window he watched her walk out to her little old Volkswagen. They would both be driving to the English Department of West Yorkshire University, but they would do it in their own cars. Evie valued the symbols as well as the realities of independence. Steven, his books for the day collected up, sat down again at his desk. It was all very well to say, "Forget the protective chivalry bit." He was of a generation to whom a degree of protectiveness toward women came naturally. It was possibly true that Evie was more than a match for Kevin Phelan. But women *were* weaker physically than men. They never advocated mixing the sexes in the Wimbledon singles, did they? Or in the Olympics? What would happen if she came up against a thug who was strong as well as vicious? She might reject protection then, but she'd damned well need it. Protectiveness, Steven thought, was a natural part of a man's relationship with a woman.

He screwed up his face in bewilderment. On an impulse he pulled the desk telephone toward him and dialed a well-remembered number. At the other end it rang and rang, but no one answered.

◆

When she walked up the steps from her basement flat that evening Carol saw Daphne Bridewell watching her from her sitting-room window. She waved and showed her crossed fingers. Daphne knew where she was going.

As she turned into the Estate she felt positively furtive. It was early October, and dark by half past eight, and the Estate was not well lit. She gained confidence as she went on and saw that the Phelans' house was shut up and darkened. She was tempted to linger and survey the collection of car parts, rusty bike wheels, and assorted bric-a-brac in the garden, but they presented mere shapes to her, ghostly outlines of wrecks. She slipped in next door and rang the bell on Lottie Makepeace's front door.

Mrs. Makepeace was not the fat, jolly, comfortable figure that might have been expected—the sort an unhappy child might easily attach himself to. Instead she was a spare yet pleasant woman of around seventy, someone with a ready enough smile (with a touch of the conspiratorial), but also with something of reserve. Carol got from her a definite sense of rectitude. Was that, perhaps, what Michael had sensed he needed?

"Come through to the kitchen," she said, ushering Carol through the narrow hall. "It's warmer there—I've been baking. And it's a pity to waste a grand smell!"

The kitchen did indeed smell good—of cakes and biscuits. Lottie Makepeace showed she had made ready for her visit by pouring boiling water into a large teapot. She plopped a tea-cozy over it, and turned round to look at, and sum up, her visitor.

"Do you bake for yourself?" asked Carol, conscious of being judged.

"Oh, I like a bit of cake or biscuit for elevenses." She grinned an oddly schoolgirl grin. "But you'll have guessed I wouldn't bother if it weren't for the kids next door."

"Do they all come round, then?"

"They do if they smell baking! Michael's the favorite, of course. Parents aren't supposed to have favorites, but I don't see why neighbors shouldn't. The younger ones tag along with him generally if there's something to be got." She shot Carol a sad look. "To tell the truth, I don't think there's much to be done with them, not with Dale or Jackie, young as they are."

Carol nodded.

"No, that's what the rumor is at school. That's what worries me so. Michael's such a bright boy—talented, alert, fresh-minded—and he's surrounded by so much . . . well, squalor is the word, I suppose. And I don't just mean physical squalor."

Lottie Makepeace looked at her shrewdly.

"Do you remember that film—no, you'd be too young—
The Corn Is Green?"

"I've seen it on television. I know what you're thinking. You think I want to give Michael special treatment, educate him out of his environment."

"No harm in that if you did."

"You think I've conceived a romantic mission to rescue him."

"I think there may be something of that. But don't you think he may have rescued himself?"

"Yes. Yes, of course, that is true. That's the miracle of it. But it's the years ahead I'm worried about. The teens are so difficult for a child. . . . It's the *moral* squalor that he's surrounded by that worries me—do you see?"

"Aye, I see. Of course, it's a moral question. I'm not a religious body, by and large, but I know the difference between right and wrong. And I know that what he's surrounded by is nasty and ugly. But look at the difference between him and his brothers and sisters. He's not taken harm this far, and it's my judgment he won't take harm in the years ahead—God willing."

They were interrupted by a knock at the kitchen door. Lottie shouted "Come in," and the face of a young black woman appeared, and then the rest of her.

"Sorry—you've got visitors."

"Hello, Selena—I was hoping you wouldn't come," said Lottie Makepeace.

"Thanks very much," the woman said, coming over and taking no offense. She was young, pretty, and overflowing with life—not least because she was very pregnant. Her eyes danced with inquisitiveness and mischief, but there was also a steeliness that betokened determination: not a lady to cross, Carol guessed. "We're just off to the new house, and I thought I'd take those roots of primula you promised me."

"Mike Phelan's teacher," said Lottie, indicating Carol. Selena laughed.

"Oh—*that's* why you'd rather I hadn't come. I'm Selena Cray." They shook hands and sat at either side of the kitchen table. "What have you been telling her, Lottie? That Jack Phelan is nothing worse than a likeable rogue?"

Lottie was busying herself with bundles of newspaper on the draining board, from which fragments of earth fell. Then she came over and poured three cups of tea.

"I'm telling her nothing but the truth. There's no need for a prosecuting council when I'm around."

"I think I saw he was something worse than a likeable rogue, the one encounter I had with him," said Carol.

"Well, you try being pregnant, the wife of a policeman, and black," said Selena equably. "If you've had an encounter, you can imagine the sort of things he says, or shouts. The pregnancy jokes I can stand. You get 'bun in the oven' jokes anywhere—though Phelan's are remarkably uninventive. The gibes about Malcolm being a policeman I can grit my teeth and bear. There's others around here don't like the idea of 'the fuzz' actually living on the Estate. But I definitely do draw the line—or I would with anyone else—at 'nigger' and 'wog' and that sort of thing. Sometimes they all get mixed up—you know: 'What color's the bun in your oven?' or 'Is he going to come out with a helmet on?'—really brilliant stuff."

"How do you cope?"

"Good humor. It may seem like a cop-out, but I decided that with him it was the only way. 'Lovely morning, Mr. Phelan,' 'Got out of bed the wrong side today, did you, Mr. Phelan?'—that sort of thing. With a dazzling smile. It doesn't stop him, of course, but it leaves *me* less drained than anger would." She paused. "It's the children that are more difficult."

"Oh," said Carol. "Them too."

"What can you expect, with a father like that? When you get kids shouting horrible or just plain stupid insults at you, it all seems so . . . hopeless. And then there's that terrible boy Kevin. I shouldn't say 'boy': He doesn't have the excuse of being a child any longer. We've had swastikas on our door, and NF and BUDI."

"BUDI?"

"British Unilateral Declaration of Independence. It's another way of saying 'Wogs out.' Subtle, aren't they?" She drained her cup and took up the bundle of plants that Lottie had left by her on the kitchen table. "It's not so bad for us," she said. "The police are well paid, and I work for a bank. We've been here less than a year, and it was always only a question of time before we found what we wanted and got our own place. We'll be out in a month's time. But think what it's like to be faced with the Phelans as neighbors for the rest of your life. Lottie ought to have her rent halved—*and* a long-service medal." She kissed her. "Thanks, love. I'll put them in tonight, and I'll think of you every time they flower." At the door she paused and looked at Carol. "But Michael's all right," she said as she left.

Carol looked at Mrs. Makepeace.

"There seems to be general agreement that Michael is all right," she said. "Maybe I'm wasting my time. Maybe I should be concentrating on the other Phelans."

"Then you *would* be wasting your time," said Lottie forthrightly.

"How many are there?"

41

"Six. Kevin's the oldest—seventeen, I think. You've heard about him, I imagine, and most of it'll be true. He's a monstrosity, and the less I have to do with him the better. June's sixteen—and if she's not on the streets already she's getting well into training for it. Cilla's thirteen—a sly little thing, one as wants watching every hour of the day. Then there's Michael at twelve. They went a bit slower after that."

"Caught up with modern technology?"

Lottie laughed.

"The word around here is that they only had them for the Child Benefit money, and only had the last two because it needed topping up. They might just as well call it beer money as far as the Phelans are concerned. Anyway, Jackie is six, Dale is two."

"Surely they must be . . . saveable?"

Lottie patted her on the arm.

"Don't cast me as Joan of Arc, lovie. I'm only an old woman who happens to live next door."

"But *six*, and *two!*"

"I know, lovie. But I think you've got to have the will for something better. I look at them and I see them going the same way. I used to look at Michael at their ages, and somehow I always knew he'd be different."

"How did Michael come to be so close to you?"

Lottie Makepeace thought.

"Really it was like he picked me out. I talked to him once or twice over the fence, and then he started coming round—of his own accord, like. My children were gone—one in Canada, one to find work down south. It was nice having him around. Sometimes I could have a word with Jack Phelan, or Mary—if he wanted new shoes, or a warm coat. Now and then I can talk them round—once in a while, that's all. If the little one latched on to me when he's a bit bigger—I can't see it happening, but if it did—then I'd do the same for him as I have for Michael. But that's as much as I can say. I think wi' Jackie it's too late."

"Jack Phelan doesn't mistreat them?"

"Oh, no. Someone complained to the Social Security years ago that the kids were being mistreated—they thought they should be taken into care because they were neglected, and were trying to strengthen their case. But Jack saw off the chap they sent round, and there was never anything in it. Mary will slap them now and then, but a slapping never did a child any harm."

"Nor any good either."

"It's the *mother* it does good to," said Lottie Makepeace, with grim realism. "You've no idea how frustrating having kids around you all day can be. No—if Jack slapped them now and then it might mean he had some standards, thought there was things they shouldn't do. The problem is, beyond his own convenience, he doesn't give a damn."

Carol got up to go, feeling distinctly disheartened. Lottie Makepeace stood up too, and took her by the hands.

"Don't fret, lass. It's no tragedy if there's nothing you can do, because as far as Michael is concerned there's nothing much you need to do. Keep an eye on him, and keep him interested, and I'll do the same. For the rest, things'll not change. The Phelans will go on as they've always gone on, God help us!"

But in that Lottie Makepeace, for all her common sense, was wrong. And the fact that she was wrong was suggested by a significant little incident that had happened earlier that evening.

◆

The Railway King was a seventies public house of brick and clapboard, drab and mean in its furnishings, ill-lit and dubiously clean. Videos changed hands round the back for fifty or sixty pounds, and the police periodically visited in twos. It was not the pub nearest to Jack Phelan's house on the Belfield Grove Estate, but it was Jack Phelan's pub. The beer was 2p a pint cheaper than the beer in the Estate pub, and he liked the possibility of picking up a fast buck on any dodgy deal that was going. Besides, the landlord of the nearest pub was large and masterful and stood no nonsense, where the landlord of the Railway King was small and tolerant. He needed to be.

On the evening that Carol visited Lottie Makepeace, most of the Phelan family were in the Railway King. Kevin was no longer living at home (to the relief of the whole estate), but he came along with them before going about his business, whatever that was. He and June, being arguably of drinking age if the police dropped in, drank with their parents in the bar, while the rest—minus Cilla, who was visiting a friend—stayed in the scrubby little play area out back, periodically running in to demand crisps or a packet of nuts. The landlord turned a blind eye, as he so often had to do where the Phelans were concerned.

And something happened that night that really made his day. The Phelans had come in and got themselves settled with a maximum of fuss and noise and threats of "Git out the back or I'll scalp the lot of yer" to the young ones. Then Jack came up to the bar, ran through a list of drinks for all the family, and then added grandiosely, waving around the public bar: "And drinks all round. What's everybody having?"

That action was so unlikely, so inconceivable, that for a matter of seconds the landlord stood there gaping.

"I said drinks all round," said Jack Phelan, still genial. "I've just had a win on the pools."

It was true that it was yet early evening, and there were few in the bar, but the landlord couldn't get over the gesture.

"You should have been in earlier," he whispered to customers all the rest of the evening. "Jack Phelan bought drinks all round. Says as how he's had a win on the pools."

"Must have been half a million at least, if Jack Phelan bought a round," said one of the regulars, who had the measure, or thought he had, of the Phelan family.

Chapter
FOUR

T ime seldom hung heavy on Rosamund Eastlake's hands. She lived in a series of interconnected dream worlds—some having a relation to real life, some wholly imaginary. Through all of them she herself drifted, gauzy and lovely, playing some part on the sidelines. When Adrian knocked on the door on the morning that was to change her life she was sitting, faded but ethereal as usual, and going through the morning papers, scissors at her side.

"Off now, darling," said Adrian, bending to kiss her. "Anything interesting this morning?"

"The Duchess of York in Australia," said his mother, rather wistfully. "Such . . . unusual clothes."

She never approached closer to criticism than that, but it was notable that most of the pictures of the Duchess in her scrapbooks were head and shoulder jobs. She flicked the page over quickly. On the next page of the *Express* was a picture of the Prime Minister in Poland. Rosamund Eastlake put her head to one side, and Adrian waited for the inevitable.

"She is wonderfully energetic, of course. . . . Such a pity she's such a common woman. . . . She can be lady*like* at times, but that's not at all the same thing, is it?"

Adrian bent to kiss her again. He no longer had to bite back any mention of the fact that his maternal grandfather had been an ironmonger. That was not an aspect of herself that found a place in any of his mother's dream worlds. Rosamund was a lifelong member of the local Conservative Association, but she longed back to the days of Harold Macmillan and Sir Alec Douglas-Home, when Conservative politicians gave the impression that they occupied themselves with matters of state during intervals snatched from shooting grouse or landing salmon.

"You've got enough to read?"

"Oh, *plenty*. You know, I'm thinking of starting the *Whiteoaks Chronicles* again. Don't worry about me, my dear. Get something nice for tea."

When he had gone and she had heard the bolts click on the back door, and the front door firmly shut, Rosamund Eastlake returned to her trawl through the day's newspapers. The haul was meager, but she was not too dissatisfied. The fortieth birthday of the Prince of Wales was approaching, and much could be expected then. She pasted one picture and a little report into the current volume of her scrapbook, and then sat back in her chair, closed her eyes, and sank slowly into a delicious but vague reverie which she would have been hard put to describe, if asked.

When she came back to the real world her mouth was dry and she thought she would fancy a cup of coffee. She had the wherewithal to make one in her room, indeed she had anything she might conceivably need in the course of the day there, but today she thought she would go down to the kitchen. She stood up, feeling slightly stiff, knotted the belt of her housecoat around her, and went out onto the landing.

When Adrian was in the house Rosamund Eastlake usually left her room only go to the bathroom or lavatory. When he was away at work she quite often took it into her head to wander round the house. There was nothing secretive or furtive about this: She often left a little something—one of her tiny handkerchiefs, a pair of reading glasses—somewhere around to tell him she had been downstairs. He knew that when the house was empty she would go around it, remembering. Today, as she walked carefully downstairs, hands gripping the banisters, the memories lapped around in her mind.

She had come here as a young bride in 1947. She remembered how cold the winter had been, and how happy they both were. He had been wonderfully handsome, her Desmond. He was her second cousin, and she had fallen in love with his framed photograph, in army uniform, on her great-aunt Maud's sideboard. Everyone commented on what a good-looking couple they were—it was quite a joke between them, though Rosamund secretly took it seriously too, for she valued good looks. Sometimes she had looked at Desmond, maybe over the breakfast table or planting those three rose bushes in the front garden that had been so difficult to get hold of just after the war, and she had been unable to believe her luck. He had never let her guess that the wound he had received at Arnhem was not completely healed, and that it would in fact rob her of him after only nine years of marriage.

It was a sadness to her, then and now, that Adrian had

not inherited the good looks of either of them. Perhaps if he had, and if he had been more outgoing, more involved in the big world, she would have . . . made more effort. Tried to get over what had happened to her. But he was a dear boy. She would not have him any other than he was. She felt keenly that there was no way she could repay his wonderful devotion in all those years since . . . since she had retreated from life.

She poured water from the kettle into her cup. Instant coffee, Rosamund thought, was a plebeian drink, but it was convenient. She would hardly want to get the percolator out just for herself. She opened the biscuit tin with the silver wedding picture of the Queen and Duke on the lid, and got out three orange creams. They felt a little soft. On the slate by the door into the scullery she wrote "sweet biscuits." There—that would tell Adrian she had been up and about. Cup and saucer in one hand, plate in the other, she started back upstairs.

At the turn of the stairs she paused. There was a little girl at the gate of The Hollies. Well, not such a *little* girl, and a decidedly dirty one. Obviously a child from the Estate. The Hollies being empty, except for the woman in the basement flat, one had to be careful. If the local children found a way in they would infest the place, ruin the fittings, and break the windows. She had never greatly liked Dr. Pickering, who had been brusque, almost dismissive, about her condition, but until it was sold it was his, and should be protected. Rosamund was very strong on property. Once back in her room she took a sip of her coffee, a bite of biscuit, then glided over the landing and into Adrian's bedroom, from where she could see the front garden of The Hollies.

She was invading no privacy by coming into this room.

It had no impression of Adrian at all. It was the sitting room that bore—faintly—that: the collection of records, the books on Mahler and Strauss, the small collection of favorite poetry, the memoirs of cricketers.

She stood at the window, looking down. The garden of The Hollies she could see, and the lintel over the front door. The child was standing at the door—she could see the horrible purple skirt she had been wearing. Suddenly the skirt disappeared. Rosamund would have liked to go back to her coffee, but something impelled her to watch on. Had the child gone *into* the house? What should she do if so? What was she doing there anyway? Shouldn't she have been in school?

A minute or two later she was rewarded by a sight of that horrible skirt and then the child herself, who came out from under the porch and then ran down the path, emitting a raucous shout. She was gesturing to someone down the road. Rosamund turned her head, and coming along Wynton Lane she saw a little squad of people: a heavy, dirty man who looked as if he had slept in his clothes for the past week; a slatternly woman pushing a push-chair and shoving forward the toddler who belonged in it, but who was instead walking beside her; a teenage girl, deplorably dressed, making a precocious attempt at sexiness; and lastly a smaller girl, maybe just of school age, but still uncertain on her feet. . . . What a gang!

Suddenly it came to her. The Phelans! This must be the Phelans. With feelings of dread mixed with excitement she watched their progress down the road. Periodically the man bellowed something or other to one of his children. Closer to, she saw that he was unshaven, and when he got to the gate she saw—her heart seemed to jump into her mouth—that he had a key in his hands. Fascinated, she watched as the family, shouting and laughing, came into the garden. Feeling greatly daring she pushed open the window a fraction. The male Phelan led the way, and as they all disappeared from view she heard, unmistakably, the sound of a key being inserted into a lock, of a door opening.

Rosamund Eastlake was appalled—appalled, and yet still oddly excited, which was something she could not account for. She went back to her room and sank down into her chair feeling quite exhausted. As she sipped her cooling coffee she wondered what she should do. The Phelans were *viewing* the house, viewing The Hollies. She could phone Adrian at work, but she knew (without his ever having been so brutal as to have said so), that he hated her to do that. He was regarded at the Social Security Office as something of a mother's boy, a muff, and her ringing only confirmed that. And, of course, he would be *very* upset, and perhaps needlessly.

It came suddenly into her mind that for once she was being faced with the need to do something—not do something to pass the time, but do something in response to an outside stimulus. It was almost . . . pleasant. A nice change.

If she couldn't ring Adrian, whom could she ring? Someone else from the houses on Wynton Lane. She had an extension phone in her bedroom—for emergencies, for if she was taken ill, though she never *was* ill, not like that. The newer people she knew nothing of, having at most seen them from the window. Only Daphne Bridewell and Algy Cartwright had been there in the days before she . . . withdrew from life. Daphne she could not ring: They had been friends in the old days, and after all this time it would be impossible to talk to her naturally. But Algy Cartwright she had never been close to, though she and Desmond had always been on perfectly good terms with him and his wife. Hadn't Adrian told her that his wife had died recently? Or maybe six months or so ago? Should she begin by offering her condolences, she wondered? No—it would look odd, after all this time. And the situation called for no nonsense, no dallyings and explanations; it demanded immediate action. She pulled the telephone directory toward her, found his number, and dialed.

"Sleate 768259."

"Mr. Cartwright? This is Rosamund Eastlake."

"Good Lord! . . . Sorry, Mrs. Eastlake. I didn't mean to sound rude. You took me by surprise."

Algy's tone had not been so much surprise as bordering on stupefaction, as if he had been rung up by a figure from a fairy tale, or by some television personality.

"Oh, I quite understand. I haven't been very . . . sociable these last few years. Mr. Cartwright, have you seen who has just gone into The Hollies?"

"No, I haven't been . . . well, to tell the truth, I've been watching the telly."

"It's—I'm sure of it—that terrible family from the Estate. The Phelans. The family everyone's afraid of."

"Do you mean they're in the garden? Or breaking in?"

"No. That's what I thought at first, but it's worse than that. There was a young girl came first: She went to the front door, then disappeared for a bit, and I thought she must have got in somehow. But then all the others came along, and the man had a key! He let them all in!"

"Good Lord!" said Mr. Cartwright again. "You mean they've been to the Estate Agents and . . . Oh!"

"What?"

"I've just remembered something. I was in the Belfield Arms the other night . . . it's somewhere to go of an evening . . . and some chaps at the next table were laughing about Jack Phelan. They said he'd bought drinks all round the other night at the Railway King. Reckoned he'd had a win on the pools."

"Oh, my God! Then it's not just some cruel prank. I was clinging to the idea that it might be. I'm just thinking of what Adrian will feel—how awful it will be for *him*."

"For all of us, if what I hear about the Phelans is true."

"Then *do* something, Mr. Cartwright. I'm just a poor invalid—there's nothing much I can do, confined to my room here. I'm going to leave it in your hands."

"But what—?"

"*Do* something, Algy!"

◆

When Algy Cartwright put down the phone he felt a little spurt of excitement not unlike that experienced earlier by Mrs. Eastlake. He felt no animus against people on the Estate. In his time he had chased children from there out of his garden, cuffed ones he'd caught stealing apples from his trees. He had a typical Yorkshire bluntness, and it could shade off (as with most Yorkshiremen) into thoughtless cruelty. But there was little real harm in him, and little snobbery. The Phelans, he knew, were something different. He had seen them as he walked through the Estate to get his paper, and, of course, there had never been any lack of talk about them. From all he'd heard they were quite terrible. And then again, this was something to do: an activity, a purpose.

He heard a noise from the back, and went through his kitchen to open cautiously the back door. Yes, they were

there! There were children next door, running and shouting in the back garden of The Hollies. To provide a
pretext he took the key to his garden shed from its hook
by the door and pottered down the path.

"Oy, oy! The natives are taking notice!"

It was said softly, but it was the softness of someone
who was mainly used to talking at the top of his voice. So
Jack Phelan was out there and had seen through his pretext. Algy Cartwright was quite short, and could not see
over the hedge. Well, there was no going back now.
Proudly he fetched a bag of potting compost from his shed
and retreated to his kitchen.

He left the back door open, though, and fragments of
talk wafted through to him as he stood there feeling—an
odd combination—both important yet ridiculous. "Garage, see," he heard Phelan say. "Stabling for the Merc."
The children were obviously taken with the trees and
began to climb them. "Come down, you little buggers,"
shouted their father. "They're not ours yet."

When the voices faded and he heard the sound of a door
banging, Algy Cartwright retreated into his house. Like
Rosamund Eastlake, he considered where would be best to
observe the front from. He went upstairs to the cold
bedroom which once they had called the guest bedroom—
mainly used by Marjorie's mother on her annual and un-
welcome visits in days long gone by. He stood there by
the window, shivering slightly, and looking through the
lace curtains. There were no passersby in Wynton Lane,
but up in the Estate there were the usual comings and
goings: women with shopping bags, the odd unemployed
man or shift-worker returning from the newsagent's with
the *Sun* or the *Mirror*. No sound from The Hollies. Then
suddenly the front door opened and out they came.

This was the first time he had seen them. First there was a girl in her teens, heavily made up, in unsuitably high-heeled shoes and a light dress of shoddy material that seemed to be the only thing she had on. "Nymphet," said Algy Cartwright to himself—it was a word he had only learned in late middle-age, but he had found it very useful since then. Then came a push-chair with a child in it, maneuvered down the steps by the mother without help from either daughter or husband. Algy thought at first she was pregnant again, but he decided on getting a better view that she was merely overweight—a heavy, slatternly woman with straight, unwashed hair and a cigarette dangling from her mouth. Behind her two girls, one about thirteen, the other about five, both of them darting here and there round the front garden, giggling and shouting, breaking branches off the shrubs and trampling late-flowering plants. Bringing up the rear was father. Algy knew him all too well, had often seen him around in the area—always dirty, often shouting, usually with an expanse of belly showing through missing shirt-buttons.

As they got to the front gate and made their raucous, disorganized way through it, Jack Phelan, in a lazy, derisive gesture, turned in the direction of Algy Cartwright's house and made an unmistakable V-sign. Algy retreated hurriedly from the window.

Now they were gone he could think of what to do. That little spurt of excitement (rare nowadays for him) remained with him. He was uncertain, though, felt the need to consult, and when he had gone downstairs he went through the kitchen and pottered down the back garden again and out to the lane at the back to see if there was anyone around. He was rewarded by Daphne Bridewell coming briskly out to her garage. Though they were not friends—

Daphne had been a teacher, a deputy headmistress, and Algy had no pretensions to learning or culture—they had all the easy familiarity of long-established neighbors.

"Did you see who was round viewing The Hollies?" he demanded, unable to keep the excitement out of his voice. "The Phelans, from the Estate!"

"My God!" said Daphne Bridewell. "They are bad news. But how on earth could they think of affording a house like that?"

"There was talk in the Belfield Arms of a pools win."

"It would have to be that, or Sun *Bingo*."

"There were four children with them."

"They've got six."

"There were three girls and a toddler."

"There's two other boys. Michael—he's about twelve—is apparently quite a bright boy. The girl in my flat is his teacher, and she's very interested in him. The only ones I had to do with when I was at Burtle Middle School were Kevin and June. *He* was an animal—indescribably nasty—and she was a tart, or one in the making."

"Mrs. Eastlake says we've got to do something."

"Mrs. *East*lake?"

Daphne Bridewell was stiff with astonishment.

"Yes, she rang. First time I've spoken with her in years. It was she who first saw them. She thought we ought to get together, I think—maybe make some plan of campaign."

"Well," said Daphne Bridewell, opening her garage, "keep me informed. I've got to go. Council subcommittee. I can see why Rosamund is concerned. But I don't see what anyone can do, if the Phelans can put down the money."

That depressed Algy. As he walked back into Rosetree Cottage he thought that if Mrs. Bridewell, a councillor, didn't think they could do anything, the situation must be pretty hopeless. He wondered who else he should talk to. There was someone in the basement of The Hollies, but he had seldom seen her, and never met her; in any case, she would be a lodger rather than an owner, like the man in his own basement flat, whom he had hardly spoken to, and never with any pleasure. There was the university fellow in Ashdene who would surely be concerned if he knew, but he'd never done more than wave on his way in or out, and had been there hardly more than eighteen months. The Packards he knew better—they'd been in York House seven or eight years, and he often swapped words with Mrs. Packard if she was in her garden. The husband—he couldn't remember his name—was manager of Foodwise, in town. He was sometimes abrupt, but he seemed a capable young chap.

Algy went into his dark little hall and fetched the telephone directory. Why was everything printed so *small* these days? He noted the number down on a bit of paper, then went back into the hall to ring.

"Could I speak to the manager, to Mr. Packard, please?"

"Who's calling?"

"My name is Algy Cartwright." He added, thinking that young Packard might not recognize his name: "I'm a neighbor of his."

There was a pause, and then a brusque "Yes?"

He thinks I'm using the fact of being a neighbor of his to complain to the top about poor-quality vegetables or a moldy jar of fish paste, thought Algy miserably.

"Mr. Packard, I'm sorry to bother you, I know you'll be busy, but Mrs. Eastlake was very worried and I—well, to cut a long story short"—Algy Cartwright was getting flustered and losing his thread, conscious of clicks of annoyance from the other end of the line—"the empty house next to me, you know, Pickering's house, The Hollies, well, today it's been viewed by a family from the Estate. You probably wouldn't know them, a family called Phelan—"

"What?"

"Yes, and it does seem as if they would be very undesir—"

"You mean viewed to *buy?*"

"Yes. They had the key."

"Christ Almighty! . . . Look, Mr. Cartwright, I'm busy at the moment. Will you do something, and do it now? Go round to all the people in the houses, *all* of them, and tell them there's a crisis meeting at my house tonight. Seven, let's say—no, seven-thirty. Tell them to strain every nerve to be there—this is an emergency. Got that? Right. See you then."

Algy put the phone down. If he'd thought about it he might have been offended by young Packard's peremptory tone, but he didn't think about it. He felt invigorated, alive. It didn't even occur to him for some time that if the meeting was at seven-thirty he would miss *Coronation Street,* and when it did, it didn't particularly bother him.

Chapter
FIVE

♦

*A*lgy Cartwright was unusually active for the rest of the day. He scurried hither and thither around the houses in Wynton Lane in a manner that rather resembled the behavior of one of those elderly characters in a television sitcom—quirky, lovable, and patronized—who suddenly discover a purpose in life: a neighborhood watch scheme or bringing up an unbearable grandchild. Algy bustled, as he had had no cause to bustle since he had retired from work. He flowered.

As a matter of courtesy he decided he should first tell Mrs. Packard of the proposed meeting at her house that evening, in case her husband had been too busy to communicate this to her. He found, indeed, that she knew nothing about it. She received the news with a smile that was slightly quizzical, eyebrows raised, and she said she thought the whole thing was probably a joke on the Phelans' part. Mr. Copperwhite (or Doctor or Professor—Algy was unsure about university titles) was not in, and neither was his girlfriend (or live-in lover, or common-law wife—Algy was unsure about the usage in that sphere too). Daphne Bridewell was still at her committee meeting, but Algy left a note in her letter box, and as luck would have it met Carol Southgate coming home from school as he walked down the path. Carol was surprised at the news, had heard nothing about a pools win from Michael Phelan, and agreed that the Phelans would make appalling neighbors. However, she felt that, as one of the Phelan children's class teacher, she really could not join in any concerted action against them, if that was what was comtemplated. Algy Cartwright had to agree, and thought she seemed a very nice young lady.

The woman in the basement flat of The Hollies was home after five. She said her name was Valerie Hobbs, smiled a mechanical smile of sympathy when she was told of Algy's mission, but said she was only there on a short-term lease from Dr. Pickering while she looked for something bigger, so she didn't feel it concerned her, really. Algy said he understood. The lodger in his own basement flat Algy would have preferred to leave out of things: He was a man of thirty-five, an inspector for the gas board—lonely, reclusive, surly. But Lynn Packard had said lodgers too, so Algy made the attempt. When the man answered the door and was told of the meeting, he simply muttered "No concern of mine—I don't give a bugger," and shut the door again.

Those were the only basement flats occupied. So it would be the householders alone who took action, which was logical since the threat was to them. It only remained to talk to the Copperwhites (he preferred to think of them as that in his own mind). Evie Soames was on the phone in the hall when he rang the bell at six, but she waved him through to the study, where he found Steven at his desk, surrounded by piles of essays, in front of him a plate holding what Algy recognized as a Marks and Spencer's prepared meal. He too was on the phone. Two lines in the one house, thought Algy, impressed. Steven Copperwhite was obviously surprised to see him, but he motioned him to a seat, while he went on talking into the phone about putting positions on ice and reshuffling junior posts. Algy preferred to stand, and he wandered around the room looking at the books in the bookcases, and then—not finding these very interesting—at Steven's group picture of Balliol in 1957.

"Recognize him?" said Steven, finishing his phone call and coming over. "Bob McLennan—used to lead the SDP, or part of it. And that chap there—"

He pulled himself up. He was intensely proud of having been to Balliol, and had all too frequently in the past regaled visitors with details of the men who had been there "in my time." But the fact was there were few notables: a good second-rank novelist, a Conservative MP of repellent right-wing views, a notable Indian writer. It wasn't much of a haul. Recently a visitor to whom he had given his spiel had remarked that it would make more sense to talk not about the effortless superiority but about the effortless mediocrity of Balliol men. Steven had been mortally offended and had resolved to keep more quiet on the subject in future.

"But you won't be interested in my college chums," he said genially. "What can I do for you?"

When Algy had explained—haltingly, for he had an obscure feeling that he had just been put in his place—Steven exploded satisfyingly.

"You can't be serious! My God! The Phelans! Oh, yes, I've heard about them. They're poison. You're quite right—Packard is quite right—to be concerned. This has got to be stopped." Hearing a noise in the hall he strode over to the door. "Evie! Do you realize the Phelans have been viewing The Hollies?"

Evie came in, smiled pleasantly at Algy, and stood there coolly—indeed with something of the same quizzical expression on her face that Algy had seen on Jennifer Packard's.

"Good Lord! They must have gone up in the world. Or was it just a joke?"

"Cartwright here heard him say 'It's not ours yet.' We're getting together tonight. Something's got to be done."

Evie raised her eyebrows.

"*Done?* What are you suggesting? That we all arm ourselves with pitchforks to see them off when they move in? The Wynton Lane Vigilantes?"

"Don't be facetious, Evie. What we're going to do is what we shall be discussing at the Packards' tonight."

"Sounds like the sort of thing the Race Relations Act should have outlawed."

"Race? What are you talking about? This has got nothing to do with race."

"Not specifically, but it's similar. You don't want them here because they're common."

"Common? They're a whole lot worse than common! They're beyond the pale! Look at what that young brute did to you. And they'll play havoc with the value of these properties."

"That, at any rate, is honest," Evie said, still very cool and rather amused. She looked at her watch. "I've got something on at half past eight. But I can see I'm going to have to sit in on at least part of this meeting."

———————◆———————

Jennifer Packard handed round the plates of refreshments to the little group, then put them on the two coffee tables so that they could help themselves. She had prepared snacks not too lavish and not too modest—delicious things on cream cheese and cracker biscuits. Lynn always liked her to err on the side of generosity when it came to refreshments, because, of course, they got all their food at a discount from the Foodwise chain. She had prepared, in fact—without being asked or told—exactly what Lynn would have wanted her to prepare.

Lynn was clearing his throat now.

"Ladies and gentlemen, I've called together this gathering—with the help of Mr. er, Cartwright, much appreciated—to meet a situation that I for one would never have foreseen. You could call it a crisis meeting. Mr. Cartwright—Algy—will have told you what this crisis is, and I don't think I need to spell out the consequences that would follow this family's moving here: the personal annoyance to ourselves; the risks to our children (I realize that Jennifer and I are the only ones to be faced with that danger at this particular moment in time, but I'm sure you can all appreciate our concern); and there's also the potentially disastrous drop in property values if one of these houses is allowed—to put the matter bluntly—to become a slum." He looked around the little group with a gaze of strong-minded concern. "The prospect is horrendous."

"You're right," said Adrian Eastlake. "Something has got to be done."

The remark was both heartfelt yet feeble. It dropped into the atmosphere of the living room with dispiriting effect. Lynn Packard repressed—as he was seldom able to do—his irritation.

"Exactly. The question is, what?"

He had been half-conscious as he spoke that he did not have all his audience with him. Now the dissentient voice spoke.

"I should have thought," Evie Soames drawled, "that the question in the first instance is not what you *should* do, but what you *can* do."

Lynn chose to treat this as a purely practical question.

"Ah, well—it seems to me that there are some avenues that suggest themselves. First of all, the vendor: Dr. Pickering. He was our neighbor here for—what?—six years. One of us could certainly approach him."

"But what would be the point?" asked Jennifer Packard, pricked by some impulse of mischief that had presumably been aroused by her husband's strain of pomposity. "If he is asking a certain price for The Hollies, and if this man can come up with the money, why should he care about anything else? Market forces rule—OK."

"What's that supposed to mean?" spluttered her husband.

"It means that you've always been against sentiment entering into what ought to be purely commercial transactions."

"I wouldn't call it sentiment—expecting him to have some consideration for us, as ex-neighbors."

"But that's what it *is*, isn't it?"

"I've always found Dr. Pickering rather brusque," said Adrian Eastlake sadly. "And so has Mother."

Lynn Packard felt the meeting falling apart. He was conscious of the satiric eye of Evie Soames on him.

"My point is that we have to explore every avenue. Another possibility is the estate agents whose hands the house is in. Another is the building society they'll be going to for loans."

"The same consideration that applies to Dr. Pickering applies to the estate agents," pointed out Evie Soames, with an obvious relish. "Why should they care? If the Phelans—let's be brave and give them a name, shall we? —can come up with the money, that's all they will care about. We've no certainty they will need to go to a building society for a loan, and if they do the society won't need *us* to tell them their business: Anyone with half an eye could see that the Phelans aren't the best risk in the world." She got up. "I've got to go, I'm afraid. But as far as I'm concerned the question of whether or not we want them as neighbors simply doesn't arise. There's nothing we can do. You can't choose your neighbors. The only conceivable thing you could do would be to club together and buy it yourselves. But *then* you'd be on dodgy ground when you came to selling it again if you tried to stop the Phelans buying it." She smiled around, giving them the aggravating impression that she regarded them as comic. "So you'd best resign yourselves to your own impotence."

There was general relief when she had gone.

"It seems to me your good lady is thinking too negatively," said Lynn to Steven, who sat there sweating and embarrassed, but thankful Evie had not heard herself described as his good lady.

"The suggestion about clubbing together is the only practical suggestion we've had so far," pointed out Daphne Bridewell, who had also registered and not relished Lynn's phrase. "Though as a retired person I wouldn't be in a position to come in on it. Neither, I imagine, would Mr. Cartwright. Banks and building societies don't rush to give loans to elderly people."

Algy Cartwright nodded. Adrian Eastlake looked round in despair. That left three householders. Where would he lay hands on thirty-odd thousand?

"There's also the question of the police," said Lynn, looking down at his notes. "From what I hear he's the sort of man who must have a record."

"I remember some trouble with the police while I was Deputy Head at the school," confirmed Daphne Bridewell.

"I can't say too much," said Adrian Eastlake, looking around at them pinkly, "because of my job, you understand. But when I had to call on him, I did some . . . background research, and he does have a criminal record. Though of a minor kind," he concluded lamely.

So what? Jennifer Packard wanted to say. What was there to stop criminals buying houses? It was one of the things they most frequently used their gains for, and no wonder, the way house prices were soaring. But she had stored up enough black marks that evening already, marks which would be brought up against her when everyone had gone, so she held her peace. She sat there wondering what they would have done if not the Phelans but an ordinary family from the Belfield Grove Estate had won the pools and decided to buy The Hollies. Nothing, she supposed. Lynn would have wanted to, though. Yet he himself had grown up in a back-to-back, with nothing to spur him on but an ambitious and doting mother and his own rather brutal sense of priorities.

The talk was now turning general. Frustration at not being able to think up specific measures, combined with

Evie's insistence on naming the Phelans, had led them to home in on the family's personal and collective awfulness.

"The eldest boy was always a troublemaker," Daphne Bridewell was saying. "In fact, he was a delinquent by the time he came to us, and that was when he was nine."

"You may remember the newspaper stories about child prostitution in the Carrock area of town," said Adrian. "I happen to know that the eldest daughter was heavily involved there—she was only thirteen at the time."

"How many children are there?" asked Lynn Packard.

"Six," said Daphne Bridewell promptly.

"Catholics, I suppose," said Lynn, with a moue.

"Christ, it's not religion makes them have all those kids," said Steven too loudly. "It's to scrounge more out of the Social Security."

He pulled himself up short, appalled. He sounded like a Thatcherite. He thanked his stars once more that Evie had gone early. But Daphne Bridewell was nodding.

"You're probably right. I don't believe for a moment that lots of people on welfare benefits have children in order to get more handouts, as the tabloids tell us. They're not that stupid. But the Phelans are. The only time I talked to the parents, when Kevin and June were in Middle School and creating merry hell there, the father made it clear he resented having to send them to school at all. Bloody waste of time, he said: They should be out earning money. Kevin was then eleven. I got the impression that if we started sending children down the mines again, or into the mills, he'd be first in the queue to register his lot."

"It's no wonder they've grown up as they have done," said Lynn. "That makes me all the more determined they're not coming here. A slum is containable. A potential buyer needn't know about it, beyond the garden. But slum children infect the whole neighborhood, and I'm not having *my* children catching the disease."

Everyone nodded with understanding, though Jennifer thought he ought to have more faith in his own sons.

"Now—right. Who's going to do what? We need someone to approach Pickering."

"I can do that," said Adrian Eastlake. "He's still officially my mother's doctor, though he's never been very understanding. . . . But I suppose we know him as well as anyone."

"Splendid!" said Lynn, with a hollow ring to his voice. He had never known a wimp achieve anything yet. "And perhaps Mrs. Bridewell can back you up." He did not notice the expression of distaste on her face. "You two are among the oldest residents here. And what about you, Mr. Cartwright?"

Algy shook his head dubiously.

"He's a brusque kind of chap," he said. "A mite short in his manner. Happen three of us would put his back up."

"Good thinking. Well, you've done your bit anyway. Now I think I'd better do the building societies. It's something for someone in the business world, and I know some of the local heads. What I can do is limited, of course, but I can *warn*. Then there's the estate agents. Who are handling the house?"

"Greenheads, unfortunately," said Daphne Bridewell. "One of the biggest."

"Yes—a family firm would be more approachable. . . . Perhaps you, Dr. Copperwhite—or is it Professor?—"

"Mr.," said Steven, with a strained smile. "Pure and simple. Well, I suppose I could have a try. What sort of line do you think I should use?"

Lynn Packard had once more to suppress irritation. These

bloody intellectuals, he said to himself: They seem to need a nanny all their lives.

"Well, you could point out that more unreliable purchasers could hardly be found, that they would have a disastrous effect on the neighborhood and amenities, and that potential sellers in the Lane in the future would hardly be likely to use Greenheads, if they make a sale of that sort. . . ." It sounded feeble even to him. He rubbed his hands together with fake enthusiasm. "Right. To work. We know what we've got to do. Let's get down to it. Another meeting to report progress here in this house as soon as possible. Shall we say Tuesday, same time?"

His enthusiasm was not infectious. They pushed back their chairs and got up to go, but Steven Copperwhite murmured to Adrian Eastlake, "Bonny Prince Charles on the eve of Culloden." That about summed up the general feeling. The terrible prospect of the Phelans as neighbors had galvanized Lynn Packard into action, but it was factitious action, because essentially there was nothing they could do. Lynn could dominate a meeting, but he could not enthuse one. They all felt sheepish rather than bullish.

In the hall Daphne Bridewell detained Adrian by the arm.

"I was awfully pleased that your mother took the initial action in this."

"Oh—well, yes, I think she was shocked for my sake. I had an upleasant brush with the Phelans in the past."

"I know. Do you think this could be the beginning of her—well, getting out a bit, taking an interest in things?"

"Oh, I think it would be very premature to hope for that. Mother is a confirmed invalid, you know."

"Yes. I've not called these last few years because she made it clear she didn't want it. But do remember, if there's anything I can do, Adrian . . ."

He pressed her hand, and they all went through the front door and evaporated into the night. Adrian went back to Willow Bank to talk things over with his mother, Daphne Bridewell knocked on the door of the basement flat to The Laburnums to report to Carol Southgate, and Algy Cartwright went into the empty silence of Rosetree Cottage and turned on the television for *A Taste of Death*. In York House Jennifer Packard prepared to be niggled at for the rest of the evening over her "cheap gibes" about the free market, and at Ashdene Evie's car was not in the garage, and the house was still. Steven Copperwhite let himself in by the gate, and spoke to the two cats sitting on the living-room windowsill: his cat Runty and Mrs. Bridewell's cat Victoria—the gangster and his moll. They were something to talk to. Once inside the house he went through to the living room to pour himself a whiskey, then went down the hall to the study. There on the desk were the piles of student essays waiting to be read, the manuscript of *The Burden of Male Dominance*, just returned from Macmillan's, and the smaller manuscript pile of *You're Only Young Twice*. That feeling of dissatisfaction, of having taken a wrong turning, of being in a blind alley, returned to him.

He picked up the phone and dialed again the well-remembered number. This time his ex-wife answered.

Chapter
SIX

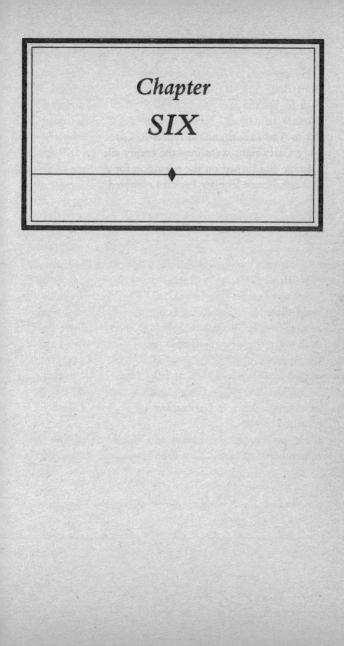

The bus was crowded on Monday morning, and Adrian Eastlake had to go upstairs. It was his day for a late start at the Social Security office, but the bus seemed to be full of early Christmas shoppers. He wrinkled his nose slightly at the fug of pipe and cigarette smoke, and went resignedly down the back.

Looking down to the pavement at the next stop Adrian thought he saw a head, a bulk, he knew. Seconds later he heard heavy tramping up the stairs, then saw in the convex mirror the well-remembered face surveying the upper deck. Jack Phelan, shaven, less dirty than usual, but still extremely unprepossessing. Adrian looked down at his lap. His heart thumped with relief when he saw someone sitting near the stairwell start to get off, and Jack sink into the vacant seat, take out a packet of cigarettes, and begin generously adding to the fug.

What was Jack Phelan doing, going into town at twenty to ten? He was usually still on his doorstep, in trousers and pajama top, first can of the day in hand, trading insults with neighbors off to work. With a sinking heart Adrian remembered he had to ring Dr. Pickering later in the day. He had been rung by Mrs. Bridewell shortly after the meeting at the Packards', suggesting that she should contact their ex-neighbor first, and then he do the follow-up early the next week. Adrian suspected that she had been put up to this by Lynn Packard. Adrian was very used to people doubting his abilities. Daphne Bridewell had told him later that her phone call had met with no greater success than a promise from Dr. Pickering that he would "think over" what she had said. Now it was his turn. Decisions, action, initiatives. . . . Like most inadequate people Adrian felt that the world was continuously calling for evidences of his own inadequacy.

Jack Phelan smoked continuously the two and a half miles into Sleate. Past the jail they went, past new red-brick office buildings with mirror windows that gave nothing away. Adrian hoped he would get off before him, but he went on sitting there, puffing and scratching himself. Only when the bus was approaching Adrian's stop, the library stop, did Phelan heave himself up and start down the stairs. Adrian held back and let him get off. Once out into Head Street he looked curiously to see where Phelan was going. Not to the library, that was for sure. He was walking heavily ahead to the lights and making as if to cross the road. Adrian looked at his watch, saw he had five minutes to spare, and threaded his way across the traffic ahead of the lights.

The handsome, filthy city of Sleate had its usual morning bustle, and Phelan looked incongruous among all the business people. Adrian saw him begin down North Parade. What business could he have there? A fine arts auctioneer, a solicitor or two, an estate agent. Hope lifted Adrian's heart momentarily: Perhaps he was looking at other houses? He followed him down North Parade, and groaned when he walked past the estate agent. He stopped to look in a window. Adrian did not stop soon enough and was afraid his reflection had been seen. But Phelan turned and went on. He was looking at numbers. Ah, now he was going up steps and through an ornate Victorian doorway. Adrian dallied. He did not wish to be caught by Phelan if he came straight out again. Then he walked briskly past, flicking an eye momentarily up to take in the plate on the wall: Simon Carbury, Solicitor.

Jack Phelan was going to arrange the purchase of The Hollies.

———◆———

Steven Copperwhite finished his double lecture on Yeats at eleven o'clock. *Tricky* poet Yeats, he felt: elusive. He wasn't meeting Margaret till half past twelve, but he felt unsettled. Perhaps it was Yeats, perhaps it was Margaret. He dumped his books in his office and dawdled down into town.

He loafed around the W. H. Smith and Austell's bookshops for a bit, looking on the shelves for anything relevant to his old-age topic. What a *lot* of fiction was published in paperback these days! Perhaps television was not destroying the reading habit after all. Perhaps people did both at the same time. Outside in the street he gave a coin to a musician playing Bach. He was always sorry for street musicians in Sleate, trying to wrest money out of Yorkshiremen. Remembering how he and Margaret had often sat companionably reading and listening to music, he drifted up to the Classical Record Shop. He riffled through the box of new LPs and wondered what she would like. The Dvořák Violin Concerto? It would make a change from the Cello. The Tchaikovsky Number Two?

Suddenly he remembered that when they had split up he had taken the stereo and the record collection. In fact, he remembered reading somewhere that when marriages break up it is almost always the husband who takes the stereo and records. How odd. Why? In fact, he hardly ever played anything these days.

He drifted down to the Art Gallery. Only just twelve, but perhaps Margaret would get there early. He dallied by the postcard stall, where the attendants, as usual, were struggling to be civil to the public, and failing. He wandered upstairs to look at Kramer's *The Day of Atonement*. It had always been one of his and Margaret's favorite pictures. Perhaps, he thought, with an uprush of sentimentality, she would have the same thought and come up and look at it. But though he dallied before it an unconscionable time, she did not show up.

At twenty-five past he went down to the cafeteria and bagged a table. As he was about to sit down a thought struck him, and he looked guiltily round. The Gallery Cafeteria was not one of Evie's haunts—too far from the University at lunchtime—but it could easily be the haunt of some of her circle. It catered to vegetarians and health faddists (as he tried not to think of them). But no, there wasn't anybody he recognized, and he relaxed. At twelve-thirty precisely Margaret showed up. She smiled at him briskly, cast an eye over the plates of food on offer behind glass on the counter, and came over.

"I'll have the vegetarian quiche and lots of that bean and pasta salad," she said, sitting down. "I'm toying with vegetarianism, not very passionately. And a glass of orange juice. I don't drink at lunchtime these days."

Steven bustled up, got a tray, and filled plates with this and that. He got orange juice for Margaret and a glass of wine for himself. He didn't see why he shouldn't drink at lunchtime. He wasn't teaching again until three. He distributed things, got rid of the tray, and sat down, grinning tentatively at his former wife. What did one say on these occasions?

"I went to buy you a record," he began. "Then I remembered I'd got the stereo. What a stupid thing to forget."

"I've gone over to CD anyway," she said, beginning efficently on her salad. "I've only got a few records, but it means I don't use them as aural wallpaper, as we used to."

"That's very wise. I hardly ever play anything now. . . . I thought CD was expensive?"

"It is rather."

Silence fell. She wasn't helping him. But—fairness asserted itself—why should she?

"I thought we should get together," he said, repressing the awkwardness he felt and putting on what came out as a puppyish ingratiatingness. "Too silly if we can't be friends. No avoiding the fact that we've spent most of our lives together."

"No-o."

"Have you seen anything of the children recently?"

"Not since summer. I went down to Peter's, and Susan

came to Sleate with the family. But, of course, you know. She went to see you."

"Yes. . . . And how have you been, then? Getting along? It's difficult for a single woman, isn't it?"

"Yes. But perhaps not so much as it used to be." A smile wafted briefly over her intelligent middle-aged face. "There are a lot of us around."

"Ah—you get together, do you? Supportive groups, and all that? Lunches together?"

"Well, no, actually." She had raised her eyebrows and now looked at her watch. "Not as far as I'm concerned. I haven't much time for that sort of thing. I'm a working woman."

"Are you?" Steven felt rather foolish. "I hadn't any idea. Where are you working?"

"West Yorkshire Police HQ, actually. Prosecutions. I'm just an administrative assistant, but it's interesting work, as work goes." She dived into the remains of her salad and quiche, and felt she ought to reciprocate with an interest in him—something which in truth she hardly felt. "What about you? What are you doing these days?"

"Oh—you know: usual stuff. I've got a new project about old age in the contemporary novel."

"Oh, good. Does that mean that your male domination thing has been taken?"

"Well, no, actually. But it's with Cambridge U.P. at the moment, and I'm very hopeful. Potentially it's very topical."

"What about the house? What's it called—Ashdene? Is it satisfactory?"

"Oh, *very*. Real character. . . . Mind you, we're under threat at the moment."

"Threat? Some sort of redevelopment, do you mean?"

"No—an appalling family from the council estate threatening to move in two doors down. The Phelans. Real slum-dwellers, something out of Dickens. Seems they've had a big win on the pools. You know me, I'm no snob, but just to see the front garden of their present house is enough to tell you you wouldn't want them as neighbors. The girl's on the streets, the eldest boy's had a set-to with . . . someone I know, and the man! Loud, obscene, filthy dirty—and as far as we know he's got a criminal record, though we don't know of what kind. I've got an appointment to see the estate agents after this . . ."

He suddenly caught Margaret looking at him closely.

"You didn't ask me to lunch knowing that I worked at Police HQ and hoping to get something out of me about his record, did you?"

"No!" Steven leaned forward, desperate in his sincerity. "I had no *idea* you worked there. How could I know? Anyway, what would be the point? You can't stop crooks buying houses."

"No. Doesn't seem to be much point in your going to see the estate agents, does there?" She appeared to have accepted his protestations, but as she forked the last of her quiche into her mouth she looked at him directly and said, "Remember that we all sign the Official Secrets Act."

This reunion wasn't going at all as Steven had planned.

"But, Dr. Pickering, you must see the terrible consequences to the neighbors of your selling to this man."

"Yes. Mrs. Bridewell made the same point. I think you may both be exaggerating, but I'd be the first to agree that the family wouldn't be ideal neighbors."

"But it's much worse than that! He is the most appalling man!"

"I've been the family's doctor for many years so you can be sure I'm not likely to wear rose-colored spectacles where they are concerned."

"Well, then—"

"As I said to Mrs. Bridewell, I would be willing to alert the estate agents, tell them to be very sure of their money—my money—before they enter into any agreements. That would be in my interest as well as yours."

"Anyone dealing with the Phelans would be on the alert naturally."

"Quite. One would hope so."

"What we are asking—"

"What you are asking is that I refuse to sell to someone who apparently can put up the money. Doesn't it occur to you all that you are asking rather a lot? The house has been on the market for—what?—nearly six months. Naturally I want to get it off my hands. Now, when someone comes along, up come all my old neighbors and apparently demand that only white Anglo-Saxon Protestant buyers should be considered."

"That's really not fair! We're not trying to tie your hands— "

"Well, it does seem exceptionally like that to me. Mr. Eastlake, I'm a busy man. . . ."

When your antagonist says he's a busy man, you know you have failed. Adrian Eastlake murmured apologies and rang off, as low in spirits as ever he had been since his mother was . . . attacked. He dreaded the meeting the next evening at the Packards', with all the fear of a low-spirited man confronted by one much more brutal and determined than himself.

It was the second time that day that Rosamund Eastlake had left her room. She hardly knew how to account for the restlessness that had invaded her recently. While Adrian had been at home over the weekend, her room had begun to feel like a prison, and she had taken the opportunity of his trips to the shops or working in the garden sweeping up leaves to get out of it and to drift round the house, asserting her presence in the whole of it. She had even thought of suggesting that she might come down in the evening now and again, perhaps have a game of Monopoly or Scrabble, as they had done in the old days. Why had she not? A sense, perhaps, that Adrian would not have welcomed it?

What the house meant for her was memories: the memories that were things of nourishment to her. Above all, they were the memories of her short but wonderfully happy marriage, though they were also memories of Adrian in childhood—grave, shy, and loving—that were almost as cherished. But all of a sudden—she could not have put it like this to herself—the memories seemed part of a continuum rather than of something that was over and done with.

Suddenly, looking out of a window, Rosamund thought: I should like to go out into the garden. It was difficult to know what prompted the thought, for the garden was by no means at its most attractive: There were brown bedding plants and dying hydrangeas, and the cherry and lilac trees were beginning to lose their leaves. Her thought surprised, even shocked her, but then she thought: Why not? The garden was well shielded, even from the neighbors. It was nearly lunchtime, and everything around was quiet. She would need do no more than put on a coat over her nightdress, and a pair of shoes. She realized that she no longer knew where her coat and shoes were, or even whether she still had any. But surely Adrian would never have got rid of them without consulting her?

She went to the hall cupboard and there they were, almost as if they were waiting for her to resume life. She wrinkled her nose at the dust and must, but took out her dear old fur coat and found it as good as new. Her husband, Desmond, had bought it for her in the last year of their marriage. A last, splendid present—though this was something he suspected and she did not. She slipped it on: It still fitted perfectly. She had not gained weight during those years of inactivity—if anything, she had got thinner. The shoes, of course, fitted. Feeling a little tremulous, but determined, she unbolted the kitchen door, turned the key, and went out into the back garden.

The grass of the lawn was spongy under her feet. Moss. Adrian should do something about the moss. He didn't like using those chemical weed-killers, but he would have to. It was beautifully neat—he had done a good job of sweeping up. The two trees Rosamund loved, even in their autumnal state. The lilac had been there when they had bought the house, but the cherry Desmond had planted. And several of the roses too. They were old now, naturally—exhausted really. But a dot of color caught her eye at the far end of the garden and there, near the gate, she found not one but two roses in bud. Late roses always moved her: so brave! She was just wondering whether to pick them to show Adrian she had been out when she heard footsteps in the lane, and turned rapidly to go back into the kitchen.

"Why, Rosamund! How wonderful to see you out!"

It was Daphne Bridewell, on her way from her end house to the garages. Rosamund Eastlake felt forced to turn round.

"Hello, Daphne."

She smiled a social smile, then turned back to resume her walk toward the kitchen.

———◆———

Carol had to stand in, that Monday, for a colleague who was sick. It was Dot Fenton, who had a variety of nervous illnesses she could call on. Carol was not familiar with 4C, but she soon realized it was the class that contained Cilla Phelan.

She only just knew the girl by sight, for, though she had been curious about her, Cilla had been away sick recently. But she was a girl who would in any case make herself noticed. This was not by any of the sort of rowdy behavior that might have been expected, she gathered, from the two elder Phelans. It was something else, something more disturbing and difficult to cope with. She might almost have thought, if she hadn't heard about the child before, that she was mentally disturbed or retarded.

It was the laugh that gave that impression—or the laughs: They ranged from a snicker to a brief burst, like a guffaw. Cilla was sitting there writing at her desk—Carol had not wanted to interfere with any teaching program Dot Fenton might have had, and had set them something to write that they could read out toward the end of class. Cilla sat hunched up, only occasionally putting pen to paper, yet coming out periodically with this odd, essentially solitary laughter. Occasionally she would lean over and pinch the girl nearest to her, or whisper something to her. She, clearly, was her friend. Otherwise she gave the impression of being an isolated child. When Carol walked up the aisle by her, she looked at her exercise book. One glance told her she was virtually illiterate. When class broke up at half past twelve, she heard her chant, "I know something you don't know," in the voice and manner of a child half her age to the girl who had been sitting beside her.

"Is Cilla Phelan childish, retarded, or what?" she asked Bob McEvoy, back in the staff room.

"Neither," he said, in his comfortable, seen-it-all way, which she was beginning to like very much. "Very backward educationally, but sharp in other ways. Secretive and sharp."

"I did wonder if she was being abused. There was a girl who was being sexually abused in the school where I did teaching practice—by her mother's boyfriend. She was very different—there was an open, horrible sexuality about her."

"I don't think there's any question of that—not in the home, anyway. It came up in connection with the dreadful June, who *did* have that open sexuality from quite young, but there was found to be nothing in it. What *was* happening was quite outside the home. She had got herself involved in a sporadic way with this Carrock business—a nasty ring procuring children of both sexes for prostitution. Cilla's quite different, as you say."

"She's just a horrible child?"

"Yes, something like that. I haven't actually had a lot to

do with her, though for my sins she's one of the party I'm taking over to the Palace Theatre in Manchester on Thursday."

"Really?"

"Yes—*Joseph and the Amazing Technicolor Dreamcoat.*"

"My God, is that going the rounds again? I saw that when I was a child. It's getting to be like the *Messiah*—always with us. At least the *Messiah* is good music."

Bob McEvoy shrugged.

"It gets the kids in, that's all I'm interested in. Your Michael is coming as well."

"Oh, good. Is this a consequence of the Phelans' new prosperity?"

"Oh, no. We have a fund for poorer kids who want to go but can't afford to. The Phelan kids always apply. It's not from love of theatre on the parents' part, just to get rid of the kids for the night. And perhaps to get something for nothing—that always makes our Jack feel better."

"Well, keep on eye on her, will you? And tell me what you think."

"Sure. Cilla is a child you always have to keep an eye on anyway."

That afternoon, after school, Carol had to go to the Burtle shopping center to stock up with food. At that time of day the supermarket there was usually crowded. That Monday it was crowded with the Phelans.

She saw them first, luckily. She was pretty sure that by now Jack Phelan had her clear in his mind as Michael's teacher, perhaps as someone who had given the boy ideas, anyway as a target. Carol had always felt that you could tell a lot about people by the way they pushed their supermarket trolley. You certainly could tell a lot about the Phelans.

There were five of them going the rounds of the aisles: the parents, June, Jackie, and Dale. Dale's push-chair and the supermarket trolley made them a formidable group to encounter—practically an armored battalion. Jack pushed the trolley aggressively, shouted instructions, got out of no one's way, cursed old ladies who were peering at prices to save a penny or two on a packet of teabags, and abused one of the shelf-boys who happened to be black. "I wouldn't go to a Paki shop and I don't expect to see the buggers here," he shouted ostensibly to his wife, really to all and sundry, and the black youth in particular, who was in fact Caribbean. Carol stayed a few feet behind, close enough to hear what they were saying, and sometimes to see what they were buying. There were large packets of sirloin steaks, an immense cream cake from the bakery section, a twelve-can pack of Castlemain 4X from drinks, ready-to-heat dinners from the freezer, and the most expensive Cheddar cheese.

It was not the trolley of a family on Social Security. Any hope that the Wynton Lane residents might have had that the Phelan pools win was a jape seemed likely to prove unfounded.

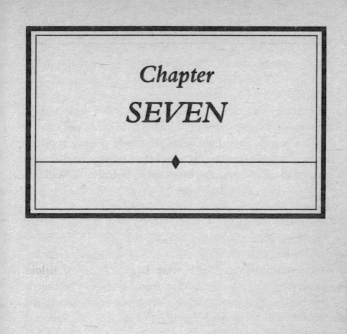

Chapter
SEVEN

*I*t was shortly after eleven-thirty that it was done.

In the Belfield Grove Estate something like a quarter of the streetlights were out of order, leaving large, uneasy pools of blackness. The more rowdy of the local youth aimed bottles at the lights when they'd had a few too many: They liked broken glass, and they liked blackness. This left the Estate an uncomfortable place to walk in after dark. Late shoppers and dog-walkers scurried through their tasks and retreated indoors.

On Thursday the Belfield Arms had turned out about ten past eleven, and the few that were still there had rolled home, most of them to go straight to bed. By eleven-thirty the lights that were on in the Estate were mostly in bedrooms. The few still lit up on the ground floor belonged some to families whose children had gone with the theatre party to Manchester, and who were waiting up, others to a few incurable late-nighters who had hired vid-eos and who sat there entranced in their flicking wombs. All were inside, with no reason to look out. The lights were out in the Phelan home. Jack Phelan had left the Railway King at ten-forty-five, and the house had been dark, bar the faint blue flicker from the television, by five past eleven.

The figure came from Grange Street and walked quickly through the Estate, crossing the road at one point to take advantage of those pools of darkness. At the gate it paused for a second, then threaded its way, in the thin light of a distant street lamp, past the looming shapes of dismem-bered car parts and up to the front door, which was in fact round the side of the house and in deep darkness. The figure stood for a moment in that pitch blackness, listen-ing. What it could hear, from a far room, were snores and the sound from a television. Quickly it dived into the pocket of its heavy, capacious coat, took out a handful of something, then opened the flap of the letter box and began stuffing it through. There was another pause as it listened—and perhaps thought that this was the crucial moment, the last chance of pulling back. Then there was a tiny spurt of fire from a lighter; something was lit and pushed through the letter box. There was a sharp burst of light from behind the glass window that illuminated—for no one—the shape on the outside of it. Then that shape scuttled down the path and out into Belfield Grove Avenue where, once more crossing the road to hug the patches of darkness, it walked briskly and normally along the Avenue and out of the Estate.

◆

Malcolm Cray was dropped off from the police car at a corner of the Battersby Road, the main road from East Sleate into the center. They had been at a minor incident in Pudleigh, where a drunk had been making a scene outside a Chinese restaurant. Now his shift was up. He raised his hand to his colleague in farewell and walked down Grange Street toward the Estate. He noted that the Belfield Arms was dark and quiet, and then turned into the Estate. He did not notice the fire then—there was a curve in the Avenue that prevented that. Only when he had gone a few yards along the Avenue did he wrinkle his nose and quicken his steps.

It was when he had started into the curve that his instinct told him something was up. As he began to run, he was aware of a patch of lurid light ahead of him. This was no garden bonfire, no precursor of Guy Fawkes night: This was a house on fire. An awful premonition seized him and he speeded up, but as he came out of the curve he saw at once that he was wrong: This was not his house. It was the Phelans'. In a final burst of speed he ran past it, up his own path, and put his key in his front door.

"Selena! Are you there? . . . For God's sake, get up, put a coat on and come out!"

His wife had been in bed. Policemen's hours are unpredictable, and Malcolm was, if anything, early. She was in her eighth month of pregnancy and found she needed a lot of sleep. But she heard through the fug of her dreams, shouted back, and within a couple of minutes was out and in the Avenue, pulling her warmest coat around her nightdress. The lower story of the Phelans' house was an inferno. Malcolm had darted through the treacherous shapes of the front garden and was now at the side door. Immediately he saw that it was no go.

"Get her out next door. Mrs. Makepeace—get her out. And get the brigade. Don't ring from our house, go to the phone box."

The kitchen door, round the back of the house, was a bit easier. Inside the smoke seemed thick, but the room was not alight. Malcolm Cray found a piece of heavy metal, part of a motorbike, by the back step, but when he had broken the glass in the door, turned the key inside, and opened up, he was driven back by thick, acrid smoke— the sort of smoke produced by synthetic stuffing in cheap furniture. It was a smell he remembered, with revulsion, from a previous fire he was at, at an Asian family's home.

He ran round the front, still clutching the metal. He found Mrs. Makepeace now out in the road, and his wife haring down it to the phone box.

"A ladder—have you got one?"

"No—but there's one in the next-door garden. The painters were here earlier."

He dashed into the garden two down from the Phelans'. Yes, there was a painter's ladder, left down behind the hedge. It was heavy and unwieldly, but he maneuvered it through the gate and along to the Phelans'.

"Can you stand at the bottom?" he asked Lottie Makepeace. "Don't endanger yourself—but there are children."

"I'll be all right, Malcolm. There's only the young ones there, so far as I know."

"Thank God."

He cursed as he knocked his ankle against the spare parts that littered the front garden. By now the flames were providing ample light, but it was difficult to find a place to set up the ladder under an upstairs window. He kicked debris aside, set the ladder against the wall, and ran up.

"Stand back!" he called down, and hit with all his strength at the glass beneath the window handle.

By now lights were going on all over the Estate. Selena's was not the only call to the Fire Station, though it was the first. As she came out of the phone box, on the corner of Grange Street, a woman came out of her house, in curlers and dressing gown. She put her arms around Selena.

"Christ, love, was it you? Were the bastards after you?"

"No, it's not our house. It's the Phelans'."

"Oh. Then they were after the Phelans."

Together they ran back along the Avenue. The fire was burning with hideous brilliance and a terrible lump came into Selena's throat as she thought: My baby could be born without a father. From the broken window upstairs smoke was billowing, but it did not have the acrid, somehow unnatural power of the smoke from downstairs. A little knot of neighbors had gathered, looking lurid, almost threatening in the flickering light and smoke. One of the men had replaced Lottie Makepeace at the bottom of the ladder. As they drew near, Selena saw that one of the women from the house opposite was carrying a crying child.

"He's got Dale out," she explained. "Your husband's a marvel."

"I know. God—I wish the fire engine would come."

From the distance, on cue, they heard the sound of a siren, and at that moment Selena saw her husband—it had to be him—in the smoke-filled window upstairs, carrying something in his arms. The man at the bottom darted up, and then slowly came down, bearing a burden in his arms.

"Jackie," said the neighbor. "That'll be Jackie."

"Please God, don't go back in, Malcolm," prayed Selena. "Come down. They're on their way."

But he disappeared again into the smoke.

Now the engine was arriving. It came from the direction of Grange Street and pulled up outside the Phelans' in a wailing crescendo, scattering the bystanders. There was no sleeping through this: By now lights were on in nearly every house. "Hurry, please hurry. My husband's in there!" Selena shouted. But she needn't have. In a moment the ladders were off the engine, up against a wall, and hoses were being trained on the house. Masks were pulled on, windows were broken. And suddenly, in the midst of all that activity, Selena saw through the smoke issuing threateningly out of the broken upstairs window two shapes, cumbrously intertwined. Her heart leapt up in gratitude.

Malcolm was big, but he was having problems. It was a heavy, unyielding, unhelping shape that he was half-leading, half-carrying. But now there was expert help. A fireman positioned a ladder a foot away from the one Malcolm had used, and one fireman went up each. Slowly, clumsily, the three men eased the body out of the window and began carrying it down the ladder. Through the smoke Selena could see that it was wearing a nightdress.

She saw too that the fireman holding the body's legs was pulling at Malcolm's arms, telling him to come out. Surely . . . yes: With a heart-thump of relief she saw him climbing out of the window, onto the ladder.

She held herself back. He would not want her to go over to him now. He was a policeman, back on duty, and she was a policeman's wife. The restraint cost her dear. She looked down toward Wynton Lane: She could see the top stories of the houses, and there were lights in two of them. An ambulance was shrilling near, down the Lane, and turning into the Avenue. But from the other direction, from her right, she heard a shout and running feet. Turning she saw Michael and Cilla Phelan.

The bus from Manchester had let the Estate children off at the corner of Grange Street. The bus had gone on, but as soon as the two children had turned into the Estate they had realized that there was a fire. Selena and the neighbor who was still carrying Dale, now quiet, ran forward to intercept them.

"Don't go any closer. There's . . . there's been a fire at your house."

"We can see *that*," said Cilla.

"What about Dale? And Jackie?" demanded Michael.

"Jackie's all right, I think," said the neighbor. "And this is Dale. He's fine."

Michael looked up at her, put up his arms, and took the small bundle. He nursed it with an odd, reserved tenderness.

"That's Jackie over there by the gate," he said to Cilla. "Go and get her. . . . What about Mum and Dad?" he asked Selena.

"Your Mum—well, she's out. We'll hope she'll be all right. I . . . I don't think your Dad is yet."

"He'll happen have been sleeping downstairs in front of the telly. He often does if he comes back late from the pub." He looked toward the house with an expression of wonder and fear. "If our Dad's downstairs, I reckon he's dead."

"They're putting Mum into the ambulance," announced Cilla, returning with her sister. "She looks *terrible*."

Selena and the neighbor looked down at the girl's face, half illuminated and half darkened by the unnatural light of the flames. It showed neither pity nor fear—only an avid interest, and a sort of pleasure at being in the center of a sensation. The two women looked at each other, but said nothing.

There was a second ambulance by now, come to be in readiness, but it was a long time before it was needed. A police presence had also got to the scene, and Malcolm Cray could get away and come over to see his wife. He said "OK?" and they stood, arms around each other, in a closer communion than words could give. The hoses were giving the house a terrible dousing. From the little hallway the fire had spread, taking in every piece of gimcrack furniture, every pile of discarded clothes or toys that lay around the place. The furniture in the living room had been a firetrap—the suite, bought secondhand with a grant from the Social Security Office, was the main source of the acrid fumes. The fireman who penetrated it finally found a man there, but the word was immediately passed out that there was no question of his being alive. The ambulance men outside had a sheet, and when the body was stretchered out through the back door it was thrown over it, to keep it from the curious gaze of bystanders.

At her shoulder Selena Cray felt her husband's body racked with sobs. She turned and put her face in the horrible-smelling blue material of his shirt.

"You couldn't have saved him, love," she whispered. "No one could."

"God help me, I didn't want to," her husband sobbed.

Chapter
EIGHT

♦

On the morning after the fire, Algy Cartwright was the only one from the houses in Wynton Lane to walk through the Belfield Grove Estate. He had had a breakfast of fried eggs and bacon, had washed up, and hadn't turned the television on even for the news headlines. Now he was on his way to buy tobacco and his morning paper at the newsagent's on Grange Street. At the blackened shell of the Phelans' home he paused for some time, listening to the comments of the little knot of spectators, mostly women with small children, and unemployed men. At the newsagent's he bought the *Yorkshire Post* as well as his usual *Daily Mail*, to see if it had anything about the fire.

None of the residents of the Wynton Lane houses spoke to each other face to face that morning, but there was a great deal of telephone activity.

———◆———

"Mr. Cartwright? Algy?"

"Yes."

"It's Lynn—Lynn Packard here."

"Oh, good morning, Mr. Packard."

"Just a small point, Algy: I don't know if you've heard about the fire last night."

"Aye, I have. I've just been past there."

"Ah. . . . It did occur to me when I heard—Jennifer phoned a few minutes ago; she'd heard about it from our cleaning lady—it did occur to me that we should . . . distance ourselves, as far as possible."

"How do you mean?"

"I shouldn't have to sp— . . . Sorry, just talking to one of the assistants. What I meant was that we shouldn't shout it from the rooftops that we were . . . well, strongly opposed to his moving into the Lane."

"Oh, aye, I get your drift."

"Because he was, I believe . . . the main casualty."

"That's right. I heard the women talking on the Estate. The wife's in hospital too, though, I gather, and very poorly."

"Yes, well, I think we should be careful, because people could, well, get the wrong impression."

"I reckon you're right, Mr. Packard."

"Of course, the likelihood is that it's completely accidental, especially granted the man's likely habits when he's drunk . . ."

"Oh, aye, that's true enough."

"But still, as I say, I think we should be careful. I

thought perhaps you could talk to Mrs. Bridewell, as an old friend."

"Yes, I could do that, though she's a woman who knows her own mind, Mr. Packard, and you've got to remember she's on the Council. I could ring Mrs. Eastlake, too. She's the one who—"

"Started it. Right."

"She's taken a big interest. She was actually out in her garden the other day, so Mrs. Bridewell says."

"Really? Well, I'll ring the son. He seems to be a bit lacking in backbone. And I'll ring Copperwhite too."

"Yes, I'd rather you rang him, Mr. Packard."

"We need to present a united front. It's nothing to do with us, and we don't want to get involved."

"Right. Pity the thing came up really."

"Yes . . . as it's turned out."

◆

"Of course, I agree there's no point in running along to the police and saying 'We were trying to stop him buying a house in Wynton Lane.' But you've got to remember I'm on the Council, Algy. I have to be very careful, the newspapers being what they are. I certainly couldn't have anything to do with *concealing* things from the police."

"No, no, I'm sure that's not what Mr. Packard has in mind. Just that we shouldn't go—"

"Advertising the fact? Well, that's fair enough. But aren't we jumping the gun a bit? Is there any evidence that the fire wasn't completely accidental?"

"Mr. Packard made that point. All I have to go on is the women talking—the women from the Estate, as I walked through to get my paper. They were convinced it was arson. One of them thought they'd got the wrong house—there's a black girl lives next door, apparently. But the rest thought it was the Phelans who were aimed at—and 'good riddance' was the general feeling as far as Jack Phelan was concerned, though it was thought terrible that the kiddies might have been hurt."

"Yes, but can they know it was deliberately started? The man was probably drunk and started it with a lighted cigarette or something. Investigations by Fire Officers take quite some time, as a rule, so I don't see how they can *know*."

"I suppose they were just assuming. All the more reason, if it's not certain yet, for us to sit tight and say nothing."

"Quite. And I can stir things up a bit at Housing and see that something is done about getting the Phelans rehoused."

"The remaining Phelans."

"Yes. The remaining Phelans."

◆

"Mr. Copperwhite? It's Lynn Packard here. I don't know whether you've heard?—"

"Yes."

"Right. It's a bit of a stunner, isn't it? Well, I've been talking to Algy Cartwright, who really started all this—"

"Ah."

"—and we agreed that the best thing we can do is to keep quiet about our little efforts to . . . stop the Phelans moving into The Hollies."

"Oh, absolutely."

"It's not, after all, as if we found there was very much that we could do, is it?"

"No. Perhaps fortunately, as it turned out."

"Right. We *said* some rather silly things at our last meeting—"

"We did."

"—but we did recognize there was nothing we could do. The question is, how many people know?"

"I was just going to bring that up. There's the estate agents and the building society people, of course. No reason why they should say anything. But then there's Dr. Pickering."

"Yes, I've been thinking about him."

"So far as I know he's not the police doctor, but he did tell Adrian Eastlake he was the Phelans' doctor, so it's quite possible the police will talk to him."

"Yes . . . He wasn't very cooperative . . ."

"Maybe we expected too much of him. It was his pocket that would have been hit, when all's said and done. It's not a seller's market any longer, with interest rates soaring. But the point is, I have the impression that he's a mite touchy, and if we approached him—"

"To keep quiet?"

"Well, yes—he might well get on his high horse. Could even talk about medical ethics, and so on. My *feeling*—it's no more than that—is that we should let sleeping dogs lie."

"I think you're right. Of course, there may be others who know. Cartwright's the sort of person who goes to pubs. He may have talked in the Belfield Arms. Then there are the people in the basement flats . . ."

"Yes. They certainly know. Would they have talked? It hardly concerned them, really. Cartwright's tenant seems to have a padlock on his mouth, I don't know the woman in The Hollies, and then there's the teacher in Daphne Bridewell's basement."

"I could ask Jennifer to have a word with her. Oh, yes, and I presume you'll have a word with your wife."

There was silence at the other end.

"Sorry, I meant your good lady."

"Yes, of course. Well, I'll try."

———◆———

"Adrian? Lynn Packard here. I suppose you've heard?"

"Heard?"

"About the Phelans."

"What about them?"

"There was a fire at their house last night. He's dead."

"Oh my God! How . . . terrible."

"The rest of the family were all right, or weren't there, I don't know the details. The mother, though, is in hospital and seems pretty ill, from what I heard."

"Just him?"

"Just him. We don't know anything about the fire yet, I mean how it started and so on, but we thought it best to be on the safe side—"

"The safe side?"

"About our . . . endeavors to keep him out."

"I get you. Yes, absolutely."

"We thought we wouldn't rush into saying anything about those. They've got nothing to do with the matter."

"Absolutely not!"

"They may come out, of course. It may be that there's more who know than we're reckoning on. And there's Pickering . . ."

"Yes."

"Nothing to be done there, we decided. Anyway, all we're saying is, we're not rushing in to talk about it."

"Right."

"So keep mum, eh? Absolutely mum."

"Not a word. . . . It's terrible, but I'm glad he's dead."

"Absolutely quiet."

"Oh, absolutely."

"Yes?"

"Mrs. Eastlake, it's Algy Cartwright."

"Oh, hello, Algy. I'm afraid Adrian is at work, if it's him you're wanting to talk to."

"No, it's you, Mrs. Eastlake. I don't suppose you'll have heard about the fire at the Phelans'."

"Oh, yes."

"You mean you have?"

"Yes. I saw from the window that there'd been a fire on the Estate, and I waited downstairs for the milkman."

"I see. So you'll know that Jack Phelan is dead."

"Yes. What a blessing . . . I mean that the others were saved. Though, really, to be absolutely honest, when I think how Adrian hated and feared that man—"

"What I'm ringing about, Mrs. Eastlake, is that we think we should be very careful about what we say."

"But, of course."

"We don't know anything about what started the fire as yet, but we don't want it thought that we were in any way involved."

"Naturally."

"It's not something we'd have had anything to do with."

"No . . . though it does seem in a way providential."

"It's that sort of talk we have to be careful about, Mrs. Eastlake. It's very important you say nothing that could bring this thing back . . . well, to us here in Wynton Lane."

"Oh, I quite understand. And you know that I don't talk to anyone."

Except, Algy noted, the milkman.

◆

Thus the phone conversations on the morning after the fire. It was a brave effort, but quite unavailing. For, unseen by Lynn Packard as he drove off that morning, unseen by Algy Cartwright as he came down the slope from the Estate deep in the *Yorkshire Post,* unseen by Adrian Eastlake as he walked up Wynton Lane toward his bus stop, a message had been spray-painted in red on the side wall of Daphne Bridewell's house—the first house in the Lane and the one whose wall faced up toward the Belfield Grove Estate. The message read:

ONE OF THIS LOT KILED MY DAD

Chapter
NINE

———————————————◆———————————————

Margaret Copperwhite was busy all Friday morning at the Prosecutions Department of the West Yorkshire Police Headquarters in Sleate. Some big cases were coming before the courts the following week, and the department was more than usually snowed under with paperwork. It was not until twelve that she was able to snatch a break in the police canteen. At the self-service counter she got a pot of tea and an egg mayonnaise sandwich, and added a copy of the *Yorkshire Evening Advertiser*. She saw the headline FAMILY FIRE TRAGEDY as she settled down at her table, and, when she had poured herself a cup of tea and taken a bite at her sandwich, she began reading the story in the lower reaches of the front page. Her interest was immediately aroused.

"Good Lord!"

"What is it?"

She looked up and saw Mike Oddie, a superintendent and a good friend. He it was who had taught her most about liaising with the detective force in those strange first days back in a regular job. Perhaps his natural kindness had been strengthened by fellow feeling; like hers, his children were grown up and moved away; he had lost his wife, not through divorce but cancer. He understood that in her case this time of loss and loneliness was augmented by the strangeness of taking up a job, after years when domesticity had seemed all that she needed. He had been, Margaret acknowledged, a brick—covering up lapses and omissions even as he taught her the work and encouraged her in her special fields of interest. He was comfortably built, with a generous smile and a warm manner, though she was aware that both hid a steely backbone. She gestured to the seat opposite.

"Oh, nothing really. It's just this fire on the Belfield Grove Estate—"

"Yes?"

"It seems to be a family that my ex-husband was talking about the other day when we met for lunch. An appalling slum family, he called them."

"That would be them. Why was he interested?"

"Said they had got hold of some money and were planning to move into one of the houses in Wynton Lane, where he lives. I expect you can guess the scenario: usual middle-class panic, action groups and all that—we must protect our children, our environment, our house prices."

"I can guess."

"I shouldn't be so cynical. I expect I would feel the same if I lived next door."

"Maybe. Anyway that explains something."

"What?"

"There was a message spray-painted on the wall of the end house in Wynton Lane this morning: 'One of this lot killed my Dad.' Couldn't manage to spell 'killed.' Never took much to education, except street education, young Kevin Phelan."

Margaret stirred her tea, frowning.

"He got in fast, didn't he?"

"Very fast indeed."

That was a matter that interested Mike Oddie. A policeman had banged at the door of the flatlet Kevin Phelan shared with a mate at 3 A.M. the previous night. There had been no problem with the address: Kevin was on their books. At the third bang Kevin had appeared at the door, rubbing sleep from his eyes and opening it no more than a cautious crack. He was wearing only boxer shorts, which flapped around his meager legs and gave him the appearance of something out of L. S. Lowry trying to look like something out of David Hockney. Even as the constable watched, the ratlike expression began creeping through the sleep and forming itself on his face.

"I ain't done nothing."

It was clearly an automatic response to any encounter with the police. The constable pushed himself inside, feeling his message was unsuitable for delivery on a first-floor landing. The flatlet smelled of sleep, and of much more. Kevin had been sleeping under a rug on the sofa, while his mate had the tiny bedroom. The only decoration the flat had been given was a swastika banner on the wall, and a large poster depicting the army of the Third Reich marching in triumph into some unfortunate foreign capital. For the rest, the room was indescribably—or rather all too describably—dirty.

The constable, eager to escape from the concentrated

smell of underclothes, told Kevin Phelan what had happened —quickly, but not without sympathy.

"Christ! Dead?"

Grief or feeling were obviously not within Kevin's range of emotions.

"I'm afraid so. Your mother's very, very sick, but the doctors haven't given up hope that she'll pull through. She's in the Infirmary. The younger children are all all right, but we need to contact your sister June."

A glint came into Kevin's sharp, rodent eyes.

"I know where she might be. I'll find her myself."

The policeman had nodded and come away.

"Whether he did manage to find her or not we don't know," Mike Oddie said to Margaret Copperwhite in the canteen as he finished his account later that day. "What he obviously did do at some time was go over and spray this message on the house in Wynton Lane."

"Some young people automatically resort to the spray gun at times of emotional crisis," said Margaret.

"I have yet to be convinced that that young man is capable of emotion," said Oddie. "Except hate, and anger, and vindictiveness, of course. Remember I've had dealings with him in the past."

" 'Killed,' " said Margaret meditatively. "Why did Kevin Phelan jump to that conclusion? It's not the obvious conclusion when there's been a straightforward domestic fire."

"It's not, is it? Though, to be fair, the neighbors all seem to have jumped to that conclusion too. Probably that tells you something about the Phelans. Maybe Kevin is just self-aware enough to get that point."

"Is there any evidence?"

"In confidence, yes. I've just had a preliminary word with the Chief Fire Officer. They don't wrap things up in quite the jargon medics do. The fire seems to have started in the hallway, just by the front door. He thinks petrol was involved—you know, petrol-soaked rags, something like that."

"Oh God! Like that Pakistani family earlier this year."

"I'm afraid so. Otherwise I'd probably have assumed that the man did it himself, knowing he was a soak, if not an outright drunk, and generally slovenly and hopeless. As is the wife, by all accounts. But she was asleep, and I can't see that either can be involved, not if it started by the front door. I'm talking to Phelan's doctor in ten minutes, but I think we're going to be treating this as murder. . . . Your ex-husband, Margaret—what's his name?"

"Copperwhite. I kept the name. I'd got used to it over the twenty-four years, and I didn't see why he should rob me of that as well. Steven Copperwhite he's called. He's in the English Department at the University."

"Tell me about him."

So Margaret told him. It was on the whole an accurate, unbilious account.

"I suppose you could say he is an idealist, in his way," she ended. "Or has been in the past. But even in the past Steven always seemed able to make his ideals square with his own inclinations." She grinned. "Bitch! I hear you cry."

"Not at all. What about this bid to keep the Phelans out of his quiet little middle-class patch? That doesn't seem quite to square with the high-mindedness."

"I'm sure it could be made to."

"And this was a communal effort? All the Wynton Lane people ganging up?"

"So far as I could gather. I don't know anything about it beyond what he told me. I rather suspect it was doomed to failure, because what, after all, could they do?"

119

"Did he say how on earth the Phelans could be thinking of buying a house of that kind?"

"I think he said a win on the pools."

Mike Oddie made a note in his little pad.

"Have to look into that." He looked at his watch. "I must go. If you meet up with that ex-husband of yours again—"

"I do owe him an invitation, though that was one debt I was thinking of welshing on. What am I to do?"

"Just pump him on his neighbors, who they are, how they found out, what they were thinking of doing—that kind of thing. Now I'll get off and talk to Jack Phelan's doctor."

He found his man waiting for him outside his office. Eric Pickering was a smallish, neat man, with a peremptory mustache and pale-blue eyes. His manner could be brusque, and Oddie thought of him as slightly Scottish—brisk, buttoned-up—though one had only to hear his accent to know he was the local article. He was not a doctor the police employed in a regular way, but he had always been sympathetic to police problems, and had been involved in enough cases to know his way around the Police Headquarters.

"I hope I'm not wasting your time," Oddie said, opening up his door.

"Not to worry. I was on my way to the Infirmary, to see the mother. Not much more than a courtesy call, in fact, because they say she's in no condition to talk."

"Yes, that's what they told us." Oddie motioned him to a chair. "What can you tell us about the father?"

"Jack?" Pickering raised his eyebrows. "Not much that you don't know yourselves, I should have thought. The man had form, didn't he?"

"Oh, yes, of a minor kind. Any small fiddle that was going—not much more than that. I was wondering about his personal habits. Could he have done it inadvertently himself?"

"Eminently probable, I'd say. It started at night, didn't it?"

"Yes. Some time approaching midnight, it seems."

"Well, if he'd been down the pub it's quite likely he came home, settled down with a can and a fag in front of the telly, and set fire to himself or the sofa. But the Fire Chief would be able to tell you more than I can."

"Of course. But that was the sort of thing Jack Phelan would do, is it?"

"Oh, yes. Hyper-inactive is how I'd describe him. In common parlance: a lazy layabout. Eating, drinking, and sleeping was what he lived for, with stirring up trouble a subsidiary occupation. It must be all of ten or twelve years since he had any sort of a job, so he can't even be seen as a victim of the Thatcher recession."

"But I hear he's laid his hands on some money recently," put in Mike Oddie. "Have you heard anything about that?"

"Yes, I was just about to tell you about it—though to be fair to my ex-neighbors I don't think it's relevant. I don't know if you know, but I used to live in a house on Wynton Lane, just by the Belfield Grove Estate."

"Ah, yes—Wynton Lane."

"Well, we moved six months ago to Marley—better area, houses appreciate more in value, and I'm a bit more out of reach of my patients. I like to be able to go down the road to the pub without having symptoms confided to me with my pint. Anyway, the house has been on the market since then. Well, last week I started getting anguished calls from my old neighbors: Apparently Phelan and family had been to look over the house, and one of them had overheard him declare his intention of buying."

"What did they expect you to do about it?"

Pickering shrugged.

"Refuse to sell, so far as I can gather. Wonderful, isn't it, what people can convince themselves other people ought to do? It was bloody unreasonable, and possibly not even legal. It didn't seem to occur to them that, after all this time, I would be keen to get the house off my hands."

"Did you tell them to get lost?"

"Not in so many words, but that was the gist. Said I'd alert the estate agent about Phelan, but I'd have done that anyway. The last I heard he'd been to see a solicitor." He grinned wryly. "I suppose I can wave goodbye to that sale now."

"You've no idea how Phelan came by that sort of money?"

"Not my business. So long as he had it and stumped up, that was all I worried about. Something dodgy, do you think?"

"They *say* the pools. He's got a history of dodgy deals, as I say, though most of them have been small. What kind of health was he in?"

"Pretty much what you'd expect of someone who drank too much, smoked too much, ate too much of all the wrong things. Oh, and never took any exercise that he could avoid."

"But there were no major problems?"

"Not that I know of."

"And you'd know."

"If he came to me with them I'd know. People get the wrong idea about family doctors—we're not some sort of medical clairvoyants. Mostly he'd come to me with minor things or imaginary things—that would be when the Social Security people were on to him to take some job or other. I don't remember ever giving him any certificate, but he got out of the jobs all the same."

"I see," said Oddie. He hesitated and then said, "I'm afraid a lot of this is beside the point. According to the preliminary report the fire didn't start with Jack Phelan."

"Ah! Well, having listened to some talk today, I can't say I'm altogether surprised."

"It started in the little hallway, and there seems to have been petrol involved—rags soaked in it shoved through the letter box, that sort of thing."

"Paki-bashing. I never thought of that. I say, Oddie, there's a black girl lives next door. I know because she's pregnant and one of my patients."

"That would be our Malcolm Cray's wife. She's not Pakistani."

"I didn't say she was: To people round there that think like that, anyone who's not white, red, and blotchy is 'Paki.' This is exactly like what happened to that family that were Pakistani earlier this year in the Armstead area."

Mike Oddie smiled sadly.

"I know. It's a pity, in a way, that we can't pin this on Kevin Phelan—meant to burn the Crays out, but managed to get the wrong house."

"He's a pernicious little thug, and pig-ignorant, but he's sharp as a razor and *not* stupid," agreed Pickering.

"Still, if he set it up with a mate who was . . ." said

Oddie. "I can imagine Kevin having mates who do all the dirty work. There might be some sort of poetic justice in that. Whoever started the fire that killed that poor woman and her child was someone after Kevin Phelan's heart."

"What does Macbeth say about 'bloody instruction'?" asked Pickering. "Somebody seems to have learned from that fire. My betting is it'll be one of the Phelans' neighbors. It's a working-class crime, to my way of thinking."

Mike Oddie privately thought that only the most slovenly thinking policeman could go along with the idea of there being such a thing as a working-class crime. But he merely said:

"You said earlier that you didn't think the Wynton Lane factor was relevant. Why?"

Pickering screwed up his face.

"Knowledge of the people. They're all pretty peaceable, reasonable sorts, however much they may howl when they feel threatened. They've simply not got the nerve. Even Packard, who I suspect was behind the moves to keep Phelan out, is the sort of man who watches vigilante movies but would be useless behind a flamethrower."

"Maybe," said Oddie noncommittally. "But maybe he could screw himself up to oily rags and a box of matches. Have you talked to any of the Phelans' neighbors?"

"Of course. I've had plenty from the Estate in my surgery this morning."

"What do they think?"

"About the intended victim they're divided. As to who did it, they don't seem to have much idea. All that unites them is pleasure that he's gone, though none of them comes right out and says it."

The question of who was the intended victim of the fire came up again later in the day when Oddie talked to

Malcolm Cray. He had arrived on duty at the usual time, where others might have taken the day off. With the elasticity of youth Malcolm had bouts of exhilaration, of pride in his own achievements of the night before, but they alternated with moments of pensiveness and puzzlement.

"I still feel smoky, do you know that?" he said as he sat down in Oddie's office. "I've had one bath and two showers and the *feel* of it is still on me. The sort of smoke it was was indescribable. Thick, clinging."

"Cheap furniture," said Oddie, nodding. "They're banning the worst sort of synthetic stuffing, but the old sofas and chairs will be around forever."

"I hear from the boys downstairs it was deliberate, sir?"

"Pretty definitely. Does that surprise you?"

"The Phelans being what they are, only mildly."

"Have you considered the idea that it may have been aimed at you—or rather your wife?"

"The idea came up. One of the neighbors in the street last night just assumed it—not unpleasantly, she was very indignant—but she did assume it. The boys who've been on duty there say the idea's still around on the Estate, though nobody much takes it seriously. Was it one of them suggested it?"

"No, the Phelans' doctor brought it up earlier. He's your wife's doctor too, he says. It did just occur to me that Kevin Phelan might have got one of his mates to do it, and he got the wrong house. It may sound farfetched, but most of these infant-Fascists are thick as pig shit."

"You don't have to tell me that, sir. We've attracted their attention now and then. But if the National Front boys are involved, and if it was aimed at us, I doubt whether Kevin Phelan's one of them."

"Why?"

"He'd have warned his own family, wouldn't he? They were just next door, with a common wall. But anyway I've thought of that idea, and I don't think it's a starter."

"Why not?"

"We'd been in that house for nearly a year. If anything had been going to be done, it would've been done earlier. We planned to move next week, and everyone knew that. Then, again, if you've seen the Phelans' front garden you'll know it's unmistakably theirs. No, if this is a 'Get out of our neighborhood' crime, it was the Phelans it was aimed at."

"Fair enough. Have relationships between you two and the others on the Estate been OK?"

"Perfectly all right, apart from the Phelans. There's always the odd problem. It's not always easy for me in the Force, you know, and sometimes I get a bit of stick from Selena's relations—joshing, mostly. Luckily Selena gets on well with pretty much everybody. Some of the people on the Estate were suspicious of me, as a cop, but it never came to anything. By the way, Selena says that the woman who assumed it had been aimed at her, as soon as she heard it was the Phelans' house that had gone up said, 'No, it was aimed at the Phelans.' "

"Ah—they're the sort of family people wanted to do something like that to."

"That's right. Or hoped somebody else would. And there's another thing: the actual night that was chosen."

"Last night? What was so special about it?"

"Normally there'd be six or seven in the house—depending on whether June was there or not. Last night there were only four sleeping there when it happened. I reckon the night of the theatre trip was chosen deliberately."

"You could be right—though it's a bloody enough crime, heaven knows, with four possible casualties."

"Agreed. Michael, the boy who went on the trip to Manchester, is with us, by the way."

"What—staying next door?"

"No—we couldn't bear to sleep with all that smoke around. Half our furniture is in the new house anyway, and everything's turned on because we've been doing odd jobs there any spare time we've had. So we just went along there, and we took Michael with us. He would naturally have stayed next door with Mrs. Makepeace, who's a great mate of his. But she's an old woman, and though she's tough she was pretty much bowled over by the fire, so we took him with us to get him out of the area."

"Good of you. How is he?"

"Thoughtful, as you'd expect. He's a nice child—the pick of the bunch by far."

"Does he know anything, do you think?"

"Not that he's so far said. But, as I say, the whole thing is still sinking in. He doesn't know yet it was deliberately started, though I think the possibility has occurred to him. If he says anything later, I'll pass it on."

"Had you heard anything about Phelan trying to buy one of the houses in Wynton Lane?"

Malcolm Cray burst out laughing.

"No! That would be popular with the people there! Mind you, I had heard something about a pools win. Chat around the neighborhood. But I never imagined for one moment that it was that sort of sum. It would need to be around eighty or ninety thousand."

"We're going to have to look into this pools win—if it existed. Will you be going back to the Belfield Estate, Malcolm?"

"Of course. We've still got a lot of our things there."

"Take the weekend off. You've earned it. Spend as much time as you can on the Estate. Talk to the neighbors—ones who've lived there longer than you have. Find out what you can about the Phelans. I know you're uniform branch and this is not quite regular, but they're used to you, and they may talk more to you than they would to one of my detectives."

Malcolm Cray stood up, grinning.

"You have the oddest idea of a weekend off, sir. Well, I'll give it a try. They may talk more openly to me, and certainly they would to Selena. I'll make sure she goes along with me, or, better still, I'll get her to talk to some of them on her own." He stood up, turned to go, then stopped and looked at Oddie. "This pools win, or this money, however he got it. It hadn't occurred to me before that it was such a *big* sum. It's a terrible thought, but that does seem to give one hell of a motive to Kevin Phelan, doesn't it?"

Chapter

TEN

♦

It was easy to miss the message sprayed on the end house in Wynton Lane when leaving in the morning, impossible to ignore it on the way home. Whether they were walking down the slope from the Belfield Grove Estate, like Carol on her way back from school, or driving down the Lane from Battersby Road, like Lynn Packard and Steven Copperwhite on their way home from work, the red painted letters screamed their accusation at the Lane's residents.

Carol, very troubled, went straight through her little basement flat and out into the back garden. Daphne Bridewell was there, kneeling on the stone path that ran to the gate, prizing out with a long, vicious tool a weed that had poked up between the flags, and then sprinkling salt on the exposed earth underneath. Carol watched her, unnoticed, for a few moments.

"Is there any point in weeding now?" she asked, curious. "Don't weeds give up for winter?"

Daphne looked swiftly round and smiled a greeting.

"Weeds never give up," she said determinedly.

It occurred to Carol that she was always seeing Daphne with sprays against ground elder, with moss killers, anti-slug powders, anti-aphid sprays, and all sorts of vile-looking chemicals from the local nursery. She must be one of the least ecologically minded members the Democratic party had. Carol had always rejected the sub-Wordsworthianism of "One is nearer to God in a garden," but it seemed particularly untrue in Daphne Bridewell's.

"Perpetual warfare," she said.

"To the death," agreed Daphne, standing up. "I don't know why I do it."

"Why do you?"

"I suppose I sort of inherited the garden when my husband left." She grimaced. "Somehow one can't just let a garden go to waste, not in a nice, middle-class house in a nice, middle-class area. . . . You saw the slogan on the wall?"

"Yes. Everyone must have. Kevin Phelan, I suppose?"

"Bound to be. I've been on the phone to Paul Dean, the chap who does my decorating jobs. He'll be round over the weekend, but he's pessimistic. He can make it less . . . glaring, he says, but in the long run the best we can do is let time do its work."

"It means that the . . . accusation is very much out in the open."

"Yes. That won't please young Mr. Packard. I shouldn't be surprised if he didn't call one of his meetings. If so, there's no reason why you shouldn't be there this time."

"No," said Carol thoughtfully. "Perhaps this time I will go along."

◆

When Lynn Packard drove, too fast, down Wynton Lane from the Battersby Road the inscription hit him. He turned very red from anger, and braked. Then he shoved his foot on the accelerator again. As he drove up the dirt path to the back of the houses, the scarlet message looming to his right seemed both to accuse and to mock. The space behind the back gardens of the Wynton Lane houses was common to all, but usually Lynn was very proprietorial about "his" space, drawing white lines around where he imagined it to be, or blocking the exit of any car parked on it. Today there was such a car—he thought it belonged to the woman in the basement flat of The Hollies—but he lacked the stomach for aggressive gestures. He went in through the kitchen, shouted at his sons to keep the noise down, and got on to the phone.

◆

Adrian Eastlake felt oddly flattered when Lynn Packard suggested that he should host a further meeting of Wynton Lane residents that evening. Adrian was used to being put down, disregarded, or treated as not quite whole. Lynn's request seemed to accord him full status as a human being.

It did not occur to him that Lynn was trying to minimize his own role as prime mover in the attempts to keep the Phelans out.

When he had heated up a portion of frozen stew from the deep freeze for his mother's dinner, he set to work making sandwiches. It was the end of the week, and he found that there wasn't a great deal in the larder or the fridge. What it came down to was fish paste, tomato and cheese, cheese and pickle, and luncheon meat. Adrian had learned a lot about housekeeping over the years: He was quite good at cutting thin slices of bread, but he found they tended to disintegrate as soon as he tried to butter them. He was coping with this problem when to his surprise his mother drifted into the kitchen.

"Mother! What are you doing up?"

"Let me help, darling."

"No, of course not. I can manage."

"You should have softened the butter, dear. Let's put it on the radiator in the hall. We can use margarine for the cheese and pickle and the fish paste. And really they should have given us more notice."

"Mother, you shouldn't be doing this—"

"Don't fuss, Adrian. I'm not *ill*."

It didn't occur to Adrian to wonder what she had been all these years if not ill. He retreated uneasily and let her potter at the kitchen table, putting margarine on bread at first inexpertly, then gaining in confidence, and slicing up tomatoes and cheese. A feeling nagged at his heart, and he realized with a shock that part of him did not want his mother to get well, resume a normal life; part of him had loved having her shut away there, his alone, to minister to. It had made his life orderly, useful, circumscribed—in just the way he would have chosen to have it circumscribed. He repressed the feeling savagely. How selfish could you get? Of course, it would be wonderful, a miracle, if his mother emerged into life again. But he stood there watching, awkwardly, feeling superfluous.

As she was finishing the neat little piles and was setting them out daintily on two plates, he asked:

"Are you going to come to the meeting, darling?"

"The meeting? Oh, no, I don't think so, dear. That's men's business, isn't it?"

He smiled affectionately.

"There's no such thing these days, Mother. Daphne will be there. . . . I thought you might like to meet people a little. I thought perhaps that now that he's gone . . ."

He found it impossible to put his thought into words.

"Gone?"

"Dead. Now that Jack Phelan is dead . . ."

She looked at him with beautiful incomprehension and drifted out of the kitchen.

"Sleate 226458."

"Oh, hello. Is Steven there, please?"

"No, he's just gone out. Can I give him a message?"

"Oh, no, I don't think . . . That's Eve, is it?"

"Evie. People call me Evie."

"Ah. This is Margaret, his ex-wife."

"Oh, hello, Margaret. Nice to be able to talk to you. Well, Steven is at a sort of neighborhood meeting. All the local bourgeoisie being vigilant."

"Oh, yes, he told me about that."

"You've met up—I'm so glad. And he told you about Citizens Against Jack Phelan, did he? I must say if it had been me I'd have kept quiet. Anyway, the whole thing's blown up in their faces, because the man they were getting all vigilante about is *dead,* and in rather odd circumstances."

"Yes, I heard about that too."

"And today we've had a great slogan painted on one of the walls accusing us. Too *Scarlet Letter!*"

"Poor old Steven. He does so prefer a quiet life."

"Yes, *doesn't* he!"

"Look, Evie, I was going to ask Steven over for a meal—would you care to come too?"

"I'd love to, but probably I'd better not. Steven didn't tell me that you two were meeting again. The poor sod's probably embarrassed, God knows why. Anyway, you two will have private things to talk about."

"Actually, decidedly *not.* I found it difficult to find things to chat about when we had lunch." The two women laughed. "Probably you and I would have had more to chew over. . . ."

They were all in the front room of Willow Bank by five past eight. Lynn Packard had determined to let Adrian as host take the lead, but as he watched him fussing around, pouring tea, putting extra cushions in chairs, handing sandwiches and naming wrong fillings, he realized that it was hopeless. Adrian Eastlake would never take the lead, not in anything. Perhaps the best thing—the most disinvolving thing, so to speak—would be to pretend that this wasn't a meeting at all.

"I thought we all ought to get together, informally," he began, easily and in conversational tone, "to pool our knowledge and maybe . . . decide on a line."

"The threat is over, that's the main thing," said Adrian, still pottering round. "I know we agreed to say as little as possible about it—"

"That option is hardly open to us," said Lynn sharply, "in view of that damned graffiti."

"That was what I was about to say," said Adrian, hurt.

"Sorry. I just meant to emphasize that that damned thing alters the whole situation. New moves are called for. Of course, the first thing is to have it removed."

"That's not so easy, apparently," said Daphne Bridewell. "It can be *lightened,* but my builder and decorator says it's likely to be visible for years."

"Years? That's ridiculous!" said Lynn crisply. "There's got to be something we can do. The stone of these houses is feet thick. They can get drills or stonecutters and simply take the top surface of the stone off. Slice the thing away. We can all chip in toward the cost."

"Here, hold on!" said Algy Cartwright. He was by necessity and temperament "near," and was never afraid to speak out where expenditure was in question. "You know why the local council don't do anything about graffiti, don't you? It's because getting it off only encourages them to come back and do it again. As long as the Phelan boy's at large and has got his paint gun, we'd be throwing good money away, and I'm not going to do that."

"Bloody hell!" swore Lynn, by now indisputably in charge of the meeting. "How long is the little bastard going to be at large, then? We all know it was him. When is our great and glorious plodforce going to arrest the little vandal?"

"Surely they'll be taking a lenient view," put in Jennifer. "I expect that's what he was banking on. They're bound to, in view of his father's death."

"Lenient view? With all of us standing publicly accused? I must say I don't take a lenient view. What sort of boy is it who, the moment he hears of his father's death, rushes off with a spray gun to accuse someone else? Bloody suspicious, I'd say." Lynn suddenly realized that a braying quality had come into his voice, something that his wife had, to her cost, told him about. He lowered his tone. "The serious question is, what line should we take with the police?" He looked around him. "It's damned unfair: We shouldn't need a line. It was nothing to do with us; we were not in any way involved. And it must be obvious to the merest cretin what sort of crime this was. Fire through the letter box—it's the working-class way of getting at immigrants. This is a gutter crime."

Carol stirred in her seat.

"As Jesse Jackson didn't quite say: 'You may not be born in the gutter, but the gutter may be born in you.' "

Lynn was pulled up short. He didn't quite understand what she was getting at: Was it some snide comment on his social origins? How did she know about them, the bitch? He spluttered:

"Yes, well, as I was saying, we shouldn't need a line, but in view of that damned slogan, accusation, whatever you call it, we've really got to coordinate our responses to the police."

As she sat, watching Lynn Packard, against all his intentions, taking control of the meeting, Carol covertly took in the assembled residents of the houses in Wynton Lane. They were all there except Mr. Copperwhite's girlfriend and two of the people in the basement flats. And what an ill-assorted bunch they seemed! Before this had blown up several of them had hardly known each other: She herself had never spoken to Steven Copperwhite's girlfriend, and she knew Daphne Bridewell hadn't either. Yet they were all three "academic" women. Nobody saw Adrian Eastlake's mother these days, but Adrian himself didn't seem to know anyone at all well, except Daphne Bridewell. Lynn Packard, she suspected, only knew people whom it was worth his while to know. His wife, though, seemed the nicest of the bunch. Carol could imagine getting friendly with her. Yet she couldn't for the life of her remember her name.

She realized that they were all looking at each other—not directly, but out of the corners of their eyes. What they had been like at previous meetings Carol did not know, but at this one they were uncertain of each other, if not positively suspicious. Behind all their words there seemed to lie something unspoken. Surely that could not be because this time she was there? There was something furtive about them, positively ashamed. Was it just the death that had made them so?

Steven Copperwhite was talking now. He seemed to have thought things through better than Packard.

"We've got to remember that some things are a matter of public record: We spoke to Pickering, I went to the estate agents, you, er, Lynn, phoned round to all the building societies. These things obviously didn't occur haphazardly, and we'd be foolish to try to pretend that they did. We'll have to admit—wrong word!—we'll have to acknowledge to the police that we knew of his intention—*supposed* intention—to buy The Hollies, and were doing anything we could within reason to stop him."

"Ye-es," agreed Lynn, but with reluctance. "We could emphasize that *supposed* intention: that we were never quite clear whether or not this was some kind of joke."

"And emphasize too," said Daphne Bridewell, "that we were always quite clear in our minds that, in the last resort, there wasn't a great deal that we could do. Really we were a bit like politicians raging about things happening in a foreign country, whereas in reality their writ doesn't extend there, and there's nothing they can do about it."

"Except that it wasn't a foreign country," muttered Lynn. "It was on our bloody doorstep!"

It was at this point that Carol was most aware of something unspoken. Steven Copperwhite appeared about to say it, then seemed to change his mind and say something else.

"One thing we ought to be careful about," he said, "is seeming to have a 'line.' I take issue with you there, er, Lynn. Nothing could be more suspicious in my opinion than all of us going along one after another and shooting the same spiel to the police, like a lot of parrots. The best idea is for us to be as various and as spontaneous as possible."

Steven's suggestion, when they had considered it, seemed on the whole the most sensible course. It also seemed to remove any point for the meeting. Though Lynn Packard was obviously not entirely satisfied, they all quite soon, in ones and twos, thanked Adrian (if they remembered) and then drifted home, to television, essay making, or feet up with a good book. Carol insisted on staying behind to help with the washing-up. Adrian protested that it was no trouble, there wasn't much, he had nothing else to do, but in the end Carol stacked everything up on a tray and bustled him through to the kitchen.

She reflected that what Adrian needed—and would need still more when his mother died—was someone to bustle him through life, possibly bustling him up to the altar first. But it certainly wouldn't be her.

It took longer than it should, because Adrian insisted on washing, and then fussed about between kitchen and sitting room in search of missing cups and plates, and all the time, in a desultory way, kept rehashing the meeting.

"I think the trouble with Packard," he said (quite reasonably, Carol had to admit), "is that he always wants a united front. Both before, and again now. As if he was some kind of party leader. I don't see why we should present a united front to the police, or why we should worry about them at all. Obviously none of us would have done *that* to the family."

"Oh?" said Carol. "How can you be sure?"

"Well, I mean, obviously we're all . . . well, respectable people. And reasonable ones. And this is a barbaric crime. . . . You're looking skeptical. Am I talking nonsense?"

"No. But actually I do find you all—the people here tonight—odder than you say. You don't seem to know what to call each other. I mean, you seem to know each other and not to know each other, if that doesn't sound silly."

"Well—of course, there are a lot of newcomers—"

"Only the Copperwhites, in the houses. And yet somehow the rest of you don't seem to *gel*."

Adrian wiped his hands and turned round, considering.

141

"I suppose it's true that it's only with this thing that we've really got together, had some sort of concerted action. Three meetings within a week! I really can't remember any time when we've all come together before."

"Yes," said Carol thoughtfully. "Three meetings . . . I heard about the first, and I was at this one. What did you actually decide at the sec—"

"I thought I heard voices."

The kitchen door had swung slowly open, and framed in the doorway was a woman. Rosamund Eastlake. Carol had heard about her. She was wearing a short, warm bedjacket over her nightdress. She had that fragile beauty that many elderly actresses have, though at first sight she seemed lacking in that backbone of steel that usually goes with it in the actresses. Carol thought she'd never seen anything so ethereal, like something out of a romantic film. Then she thought that this had probably more to do with Mrs. Eastlake's reputation than her actual appearance. It struck her that Mrs. Eastlake seemed now to be drifting back into life, just as earlier she had drifted out of it.

Adrian bustled forward, wiping his hands.

"Mother, should you be up? It's getting quite chilly outside."

Rosamund Eastlake did not reply, but looked at Carol.

"Oh, this is Carol Southgate—"

The two women smiled and shook hands. Mrs. Eastlake's hand was warm and strong, but uncertain. Carol wondered just how many hands she had shaken in the last few years.

"Oh, yes, and you are?—"

"From The Laburnums," Adrian put in quickly. "The basement flat in Daphne's."

"Oh yes. . . . You really shouldn't be helping with the washing-up."

"That's quite all right. It's pretty much done now."

"I would have come down to help. I seem to be . . . much stronger these days. Don't I, Adrian?"

"You do, darling. That doesn't mean you should overdo things."

"You must come again," Rosamund said, turning back to Carol. "When I feel up to cooking again. I used to be quite a good cook, didn't I, Adrian?"

"Wonderful, darling."

"I must get the old books out, look up things I used to like making."

She had drifted back to the door again, but at it she turned and looked straight at Carol.

"Do be careful, won't you?"

Then she went out into the hall, and they heard her slowly mounting the stairs.

Chapter
ELEVEN

♦

The Crays could not decide whether to take Michael Phelan with them when they went back to the Estate on the following Saturday, but the problem was solved by his showing signs of reluctance. Finally he said, "I don't want to go back, not yet," and that settled it. They didn't like leaving him alone, but he was such a self-contained boy, so quietly assured, that they thought it would be all right. Anyway, said Malcolm, it was silly to treat him with a protectiveness he had certainly never known at home.

So they drove off, hardly more eager themselves. When they drew up outside their old house the acrid smell was still insistent, penetrating. They got out and stood looking at the burned-out wreck of the Phelans' house—a blackened skull with charred and gaping holes for eyes. It sat perfectly aptly in the chaos of rubbish that was their garden, guarded now by a uniformed constable, to whom

Malcolm raised his hand in greeting. Their own house, the other half of the same structure, was not in any way a sentimental object for them, but it held memories of their first months of marriage. They stood for a moment on the pavement holding hands. Then they went in.

There was nothing damaged, of course. The fire had not been able to spread through the connecting wall, and all the destruction was on the Phelans' side. But there was a sort of damage in the insidious smell, that smell both stifling and unnatural which Malcolm had met in fighting the fire, and which now seemed to have penetrated their armchairs, the linen cupboard, their clothes.

"I wish we could get rid of our things and start again from nothing," Selena said.

"What, with the mortgage rate going sky-high?" said Malcolm, with a briskness he did not feel. "A lot of dry cleaning is about the best we'll be able to do."

"They all smell . . . sort of bitter."

"Maybe we could do a swap with a secondhand furniture shop," suggested Malcolm. "A job-lot of our rubbish in exchange for a job-lot of theirs."

They began collecting together odds and ends in the plastic bags they used for rubbish, piling them up one by one near the front door. Malcolm had arranged for a medium-sized van to come in the afternoon. Selena, gathering up their ornaments and their little vases from off the fireplace, paused.

"I'm remembering all the things we heard from next door."

"Oh, God, yes."

It had made, over the months, an additional bond between them. Rows, fights, drunken laughter, incredibly loud television, stereo turned up to torture levels, racial insults aimed at Selena, screams at the children, drunken songs—the tapestry of Phelan life, now brutally unwoven. Nothing, presumably, would restore that life to what it had been. Jack Phelan had been its hideous lynchpin.

"I still wish—" said Malcolm.

"What?"

"Difficult to find a way of putting it: I wish I could have found it in me to want to save him, regret not being able to . . ."

"He'd not have thanked you," said Selena, and they looked at each other and laughed.

"No, I don't think thanks were in his repertoire."

When they had collected up the smallest things, Malcolm sent Selena off to talk to the neighbors.

"I'm going to collect up the heavier stuff close to the doors, and I don't want you helping—"

"In my condition?"

"Exactly."

Selena raised her eyebrows, but went. Malcolm went about his shiftings quietly and methodically. They had little enough left in the upstairs rooms, and only the bed was really awkward. In the bedroom he paused. He had always thought these houses should have a built-in neon sign over the bed: MAKE LOVE QUIETLY. But in fact the senior Phelans' bedroom had not shared a common wall with theirs, and the noises Malcolm remembered from their early days there were from the older girls, June and Cilla: vacuous laughter, quarrels about items of makeup, silly giggles leading to hushed confidences. Odd to think that the pleasant, quiet boy now living with them had grown up with Cilla, June, and Kevin, had shared all their experiences.

When Malcolm had got the few big pieces of furniture

they possessed ready for the removal van, he decided to go in and beg a cup of tea from Mrs. Makepeace.

◆

"I've got both Jackie and Dale," said the neighbor who had stood on the street with Selena on the night of the fire. She ushered her through the poky hallway into the living room, which was cheerful and pleasantly untidy, in the way that rooms that children use ought to be. The neighbor's name was Jean Bryson, and she had two children of her own. "There didn't seem to be anyone else willing to take them on," she explained. "At the moment they're a bit subdued, so they're not much trouble. I wouldn't want it to go on too long."

They stood at the window, looking out at the back garden, in which the four children were playing, happily enough.

"Have you heard how their mother is?" Selena asked.

"No—I was just going to ask you. I thought your bloke might have heard."

"Nothing since yesterday morning. She was pretty bad then. I suppose you're anxious to get rid of them?"

Mrs. Bryson grinned conspiratorially.

"Like I said, I wouldn't want it to go on too long. They're Phelans, and they won't be subdued forever. You don't get the full flavor, having Michael. He's a changeling."

"I got the full flavor living next door. What about grandparents? Couldn't they take them?"

"There aren't any that I know of—unless old Mrs. Coppins is still alive, and she'll be in a home somewhere if she is. Last time she was round here—Christmastime it was, three or four years ago—she came out into the street after Christmas dinner and started dancing around and undressing herself. Jack stood at the gate egging her on, if you'll believe it. Mary did at least have the decency to go and take her inside."

The two women sat down in armchairs, intent on a good natter.

"No Phelans left alive then?" Selena asked.

"No. Beer and fags buried them years ago."

"Were both the Phelans from round here?"

"He was from The Wattles—council estate on t'other side of Burtle Park—but he went to school at Burtle Middle when it was still the Secondary Modern. I know because I was there ten years later and he was still a legend. Teachers used to throw his name around, to prove that however rowdy and mean we might get, they'd had Jack Phelan in their time and they weren't impressed. Mary was five or six years younger than Jack, so they wouldn't have overlapped in Burtle Secondary. It was quite a bit later when he knocked her up and they had to get married."

"A bit uncharacteristic that, I'd have thought."

"Getting married because the lass was pregnant? No, you did in them days."

"What, in the permissive sixties?"

"I think permissiveness took a hell of a time filtering down to Sleate. . . . But, of course, you're right: If it hadn't suited Jack he wouldn't have married her. The fact was, his parents were getting past it, and he could see the time coming when they'd be beyond cooking and providing for him. He just had the occasional laboring job and was generally an encumbrance, so the cooking and providing were getting more and more reluctant as he grew older. So he and Mary teamed up—one as bad as the other, but at least he got his clothes washed now and again, I suppose, and a meal cooked."

"Is that when they moved here?"

"Not quite. They came from a high-rise round Whateley way somewhere. That was a year or two later, when Kevin was a toddler and June was on the way."

"I always thought Kevin was the worst thing about them," said Selena, shivering.

"He is that. When he was small he was like some malicious imp from a fairy story, and it's developed year by year since then. If you want to find out about Kevin— you are asking questions for Malcolm, aren't you?—"

Selena felt embarrassed.

"Well, in a way. The police are anxious to get a bit of background. Not everyone around the Estate is willing to talk to the police. I can understand. I used to feel like that myself—probably still would, if I hadn't married Malcolm."

"Well, I'll tell you who you could talk to. It's Mrs. Thornton, down on the corner with Grange Street. The little girl next door to her, Gail Mattingley, she's Cilla Phelan's best friend. Cilla's been staying there since the night of the fire. And Gail's elder brother is Kevin Phelan's best mate—partner in crime—call it what you like. In fact, I think the two of them are sharing a flat at the moment. The mother's thick as two planks, and silly with it—no use talking to her. But the next-door neighbor, Betty Thornton, she knows all there is to know about the Phelan kids. Had 'em up to *here,* one way or another, over the years. If it's background to the Phelans you want, it's her you should go and have a word with."

As Malcolm Cray went out the front door of his old home, the acrid smell from next door overwhelmed him. The police constable who was standing sentry at and around the Phelan home, bored out of his mind as men are doing such necessary jobs, strolled down to the gate as Malcolm passed.

"It was you as saved them last night, wasn't it, Malcolm?"

"Yes. Those that were saved."

"You'd never have got the father out. It's incredible in there. Want to have a look round?"

Impelled by he knew not what unhealthy curiosity, Malcolm nodded.

The hallway inside the front door was a charred ruin, with heaps of what probably had once been clothing, now quite unrecognizable, lying around on the floor. The kitchen was nearly as bad: There had been a chip-pan full of oil on the stove, no doubt a permanent feature, and this had rendered that corner an inferno which now held skeletal shapes of stove and cupboard only. Scattered around were burned food packages, tins twisted out of shape, blackened plates with charred scraps of food on them. There was a little box room off from the hall which had apparently served as a bedroom: The shape of an old mattress could be made out on the floor, and the charred remnants of clothes, a few books, and toys.

"The middle girl slept here," said the constable. "You can tell by the size of the clothes."

"I thought I hadn't heard her and her sister recently," said Malcolm.

Inside the living room the mess was indescribable. Being further from the source of the fire, the flames had taken less firm hold here, though the chair in front of the television set was a collapsed ruin.

"They say he'd've been dead well before that happened,"

said the constable, who seemed to get a ghoulish pleasure from acting as tour guide. "Fumes. In fact, the firemen got to him just as the chair was going up. Foam filling. That old sofa's horsehair, so it's not so bad."

Around the room, on every surface and scattered all over the floor, were the detritus of family living, grotesquely blackened: baby clothes, disposable nappies, toy trains, a skateboard, a picture book, an old wooden jigsaw, cans of beer and soft drinks, a melted chocolate bar. Just getting around this room must have been hazardous, so that one would have thought it simpler and more labor-saving to do a quick cleanup now and again. That had not been Mary Phelan's view, apparently.

"Want to see upstairs?" asked the constable.

"No, thanks," said Malcolm, escaping. "I've seen upstairs."

Lottie Makepeace, back in her home, but still feeling a bit groggy and upset, was very pleased to see him. "You're a hero round here, that's what you are," she said, happy to participate in his local fame. She had the partiality of a woman of her generation for a well-set-up young male. In no time he was sitting at her kitchen table, where his wife had sat not two weeks before. Lottie loved her kitchen, and Malcolm could see her point: The little room seemed to hold the essence of bakings and fryings stretching far back into the past. But there was a present smell as well— that of a sponge cake, currently sitting in the oven. Malcolm was still stirring his tea and enjoying the warmth and the smell when Lottie looked at him and said:

"And are you on duty or off, young man?"

He looked at her sharply, then shifted in his chair and smiled.

"Off. But I wouldn't want you to think that anything you say will be off the record."

"That's what I thought. You can't put one over on me, young man. You didn't come here because you didn't have the makings of a cup of tea in your old home, and you didn't even come to see how I was. You came to pick my old brains about Jack Phelan."

"That's right. All the Phelans. And the Estate."

"Ah—you're looking for a motive. But you've got a problem there, Selena's man, and you don't need me to tell you what it is. There was no one round here could stand him, nor his family."

"I know that. So does the officer in charge. Too many motives, that's the problem. But are they really motives? I know all about the general dislike and distrust—couldn't help knowing, living next door to him. But what I'm after is something special, something worth killing for. Tell me, were you living in this house when they moved in next door?"

"Oh, aye. My Tom was working at the Sleate Infirmary, and I did odd mornings at the newsagent's in Battersby Road. In fact, our Linda would still have been at school."

"So you wouldn't have welcomed the Phelans as neighbors?"

She looked straight at him.

"Worst thing that ever happened to this Estate. We'd all jogged along quite happily till then."

"That must have been fifteen or twenty years ago. What was he like then?"

"Same as he was when you knew him. He never changed, only . . . ripened, you might say. He'd got everybody's back up first week they were here, and things only went downhill after that. He just enjoyed the hostility—flourished on it."

"You're not trying to paint a rosy picture, anyway."

"Why should I? We'd all lived with him for years.

You'd best be asking yourself why someone on the Estate should want to kill him *now*."

"We are, we are," said Malcolm. He frowned. "Why do you think he so loved putting people's backs up?"

Lottie Makepeace pondered.

"I think it was pure mischief. Or impure mischief, malicious mischief. What's that word that teachers use about kids? Disruptive, that's it. I think he was naturally disruptive. He couldn't stand things being peaceful and pleasant and jogging along nicely. He loved fights, slanging matches, noise, breaking furniture—and he really liked hurting people too. He was like a football hooligan grown up—a nasty schoolboy all his life. If he'd been alone that would have been his business, but he had a family . . . ."

"You feel bitter about him, don't you?"

She sipped her tea.

"This was a good place to live until he came. But it's not just that. He gave people an excuse, you see. . . . There's a nasty spirit about—a mean spirit that enjoys kicking the helpless, and taking away from the really poor what little they've got. It hasn't been as bad as this since I was a girl. I don't feel ashamed at being poor. My Tom worked at the Infirmary almost all his life—wheeled patients around, humped machinery from here to there, took the dead to the mortuary. He brought precious little home for it, but I'm not ashamed for that. I'm proud. But there's plenty want to make me hang my head because we never did better. And it's people like Jack Phelan who provide them with their excuse: Look at the poor, they say, and point to him—shiftless, dirty, lying, work-shy. And there's nobody to point out that there are a hundred decent souls for every Jack Phelan you see around."

Malcolm nodded sadly.

"So you think it was mischief made Jack Phelan tick?"

Lottie Makepeace nodded.

"Yes, he wanted to make mischief. And that usually meant riling people. If he'd had a car he'd have been the one who drives through puddles at high speed and sprays the people on the pavement with muddy water. Some do that because they don't give a damn about other people, others because they really get a kick out of playing dirty tricks on people. Jack Phelan was the last sort."

Malcolm said, "Well, he's done it once too often."

"You're right there. You realize Kevin's a chip off the old block—a joker too? Only with him any element of fun there might have been in Jack—and there wasn't much—has disappeared, and just the viciousness is left."

At the door, as he was going, Malcolm paused.

"I wonder—do you think Jack Phelan really did have that win on the pools?"

She looked at him shrewdly.

"If he'd had that sort of win—I mean a win of fifty thousand, a hundred thousand, which is what he'd have needed if he was going to buy Dr. Pickering's house—what do you think would be the first thing he'd do?"

Malcolm considered.

"Broadcast it around?"

" 'Course he would. The moment he'd checked his coupon and realized it was a big win. He'd have been out in the street, in the shops, down the pub, bragging about it. The man was a loudmouth. Instead of which he quietly—quietly *for Jack*—buys drinks all round at the Railway King later in the week. No—if he had a win it was a small one, and he was playing his tricks as usual."

Malcolm nodded.

"Jack Phelan's final jape."

Selena, when she came to Mrs. Thornton's house, on the edge of the Estate where it turned into Grange Road, found she knew the woman. It was she who had talked to her on the night of the fire, and assumed Selena was its intended victim. She was welcomed in, and the two of them had a good gossip about the fire, Jack's death, the probability of arson, eventually getting round to the family in general.

"It sounds heartless, but everyone around here is hoping the family'll be rehoused on another estate," Mrs. Thornton said, offering a plate of brightly iced cream cakes. "The fact that Jack has gone doesn't make the rest of the Phelans into the sort of people you'd want as neighbors. Well, you'd know that as well as anyone."

"I hear you've had more than your fill of the children," said Selena, munching.

Mrs. Thornton raised her eyebrows.

"I have that. And it's all due to that woman next door. Maggie Mattingley's as silly as a wet hen. All those years that Kevin was best mates with her Jason, leading him astray from the word 'Go,' and all she could ever say was 'Boys will be boys!' Kevin Phelan! Who everybody knew was a vicious little beast. Now they've got a flat together, and a right lot of mayhem they'll be creating, I'll be bound! So, not content with that, Maggie Mattingley's letting the same thing happen all over again. Now it's Cilla and her Gail. Cilla's staying with them at the moment. If I speak to the mother over the back fence it's 'Wasn't it terrible about poor Jack?' and 'Aren't children

lovely together and isn't it a pity they have to grow up?'
She wants her head reading. Imagine a world of children,
especially a world of Cilla Phelans." She got up and went
over to the sitting room window. "They're out there now.
Do they strike you as angelic children?"

Selena came over and looked out into the neighboring
garden. Two girls were playing there, both rather lumpish
thirteen-years-olds. Cilla she recognized; the other gave
her the impression of being a Cilla in the making. There
was about them nothing of the nascent sexuality which
might have been expected, and which certainly was a
feature of the oldest sister, June. These two skipped, ran
around in the overgrown grass, had mock fights. But
mostly they stood around, talking, whispering, snigger-
ing. That was hardly unusual in adolescent girls, and Selena
found it difficult to pin down the uncomfortable impression they gave the observer: Perhaps it was the expressions
on their faces as they whispered and sniggered—gloating,
ravenous, relishing.

"Awful to say this, about *children*," said Mrs. Thornton,
"but they always remind me of slugs—slugs when they lie
there on the path, all fattened up."

"They look sort of . . . corrupt," said Selena at last.

"That's it! That's the word! It was the same with Kevin,
only there it was more open. . . . And the silly bitch next
door looks at those two out there and says: 'Poor little
mite, isn't it wonderful she can still laugh and play when
she's lost her Daddy?' Some people seem to have lost all
their sense of . . ."

"Evil?"

"Yes. Something like that. Yes, I suppose that's the
word."

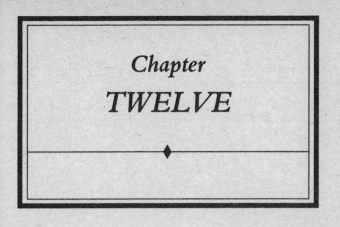

Chapter
TWELVE

◆

Superintendent Oddie had thoroughly researched the background of Kevin Phelan before he went along to talk to him: He knew his record, he knew his associates, and he even knew a bit about the house in which he lived. This was a decaying Victorian property in the Kirkby district of Sleate, whose landlord lived next door. He was an elderly and unsavory right-wing fanatic who had lived much of his life on the windy side of the law, profiting by the ambiguities of that gray area where free speech shades off into downright intimidation. Two years previously he had acquired the house next to his own, when the owners had defaulted on their mortgage repayments, and he had turned it into a collection of bedsitters and flatlets ranging from the dingy to the downright squalid. He had let them mainly to young sympathizers with his own views, hence Kevin Phelan's surprising independence from his family.

The landlord did not let politics interfere with his right to collect rents from his tenants, so presumably Kevin Phelan and his flatmate, Jason Mattingley, had somehow the means of paying it. Whether these means had been acquired by exploiting loopholes in the Social Security rules, in the approved Phelan tradition, or by some less legal means Oddie had not yet discovered.

Kevin Phelan's record could have been used as a textbook example of the early career of the archetypal criminal thug. His schooldays had been as spectacular as his father's: No fewer than five of his teachers had called for police protection from him. He had been charged with maliciously wounding a fellow pupil—an Indian boy two years younger than himself. His persecution of this boy had been so vicious and so long-lasting that it had created its own reaction: The boy had acquired a whole army of protectors from among his own schoolfellows, so that he seldom had to go anywhere alone. Kevin Phelan had been frustrated, for he preferred attacking the weak and solitary.

Since leaving school he had been prominent in football thuggery (the Sleate football ground was a notorious recruiting shop for the National Front, and black players were barbarously treated by the parts of the stands where the thugs congregated, a fact to which the management board of Sleate United turned a decorous blind eye). The Saturday night fracas, the concerted racial intimidation, and one suspected grievous bodily harm charge were the main components of Kevin's adult form. It was fairly clear, however, that he was an accomplished shoplifter and a specialist in the quick theft of salable items like TVs and videos from people's homes, though such lightning burglaries were so commonplace in a crime-ridden Britain that the police could give them little attention, so they had never got a case against him which they thought they could make stick. These were the bare bones of his record. Comments by policemen who had interviewed him were unprintable.

Oddie took two men with him to Kirkby, on the principle of safety in numbers. They left their car a street away and walked to Kevin's abode, 14 Market Street. There was no market now, though on the main road just down from the house there was a fish and chip shop, a newsagent's, and a bookmaker's. Kirkby had always been a working-class rising to lower-middle-class area of Sleate. In its time Market Street had been one of the "better" areas: There were patches of green and a church which looked as if it had once seen substantial congregations and fair pickings in the collection box. The area had started going downhill, though, long before the advent of Kevin Phelan and Jason Mattingley had set the seal on the process. They were below the present social mix, presages of some future rock bottom.

The three men approached the house slowly, casually. Oddie spoke under his breath to Sergeant Stokes and Detective P. C. Bramley, who were on either side of him.

"Nice house, once. Built around 1890, I'd say. No garage, of course. But there is a path from the front round to the back. There may be some kind of garden shed back there. Will you take that, Bramley? Especially keep an eye out for any petrol or paraffin there may be there, or signs that anything like that has been there until recently. Get down on your bloody hands and knees and sniff like a beagle if necessary. We'll take Prince Charming himself, Stokes."

The main door to the house could be opened from outside, and inside each room had been fitted with a Yale lock. None of the residents, probably, had much to lose. In the hallway the two men paused and got their bearings: The place was predictably fusty, and there hung about it lodging-house smells of baked beans cooked on gas rings, stale sleep, and horsehair armchairs. The stairs were uncarpeted, so their approach to the first-floor flatlet could not be kept quiet. There were two names on the door, but no doorbell. When they banged there was an interval before it opened, but no sound of footsteps. The boy who opened it was not Kevin Phelan, but his friend Jason Mattingley.

"Hello," he said. "Come on in."

It was friendly, or at least it attempted to be ingratiating. He was a heavier version of Kevin—fleshier, with better shoulders. His hair was cropped, his hands and neck tattooed, and though his face wore habitually an aggressive expression, it battled with a contrary expression of vacancy. Oddie immediately had a strong sense of the boy having been taken over, used.

The two policemen went into the room. Oddie had heard about this room from the constable who had brought the news in the middle of the night to Kevin Phelan. It would be too much to say that it had been transformed, but it certainly had been inexpertly cleaned up. There were no stray garments, no unwashed cups or plates; the bedclothes from the ancient sofa had been put away, and the poster of triumphant Nazi troops had been taken down. The room had been comprehensively aired, so that only faint traces of its unwholesome smells lingered. Oddie had a strong sense of unreality.

He also had a strong sense of being expected, of this

encounter being staged, at least in intention. As they came in through the door Jason Mattingley had looked out, expecting a third policeman; Kevin Phelan was seated at the little dining table over by the wall, and nodded at their entrance with a feint at amiability; the old sofa and armchair were arranged in a sort of group for interview purposes, though Oddie noted that from none of them could one get a very good view of Kevin Phelan. They were expected, had been seen coming—that was understandable. The boys were concerned to make as good an impression as possible—that was not. Making a good impression was as foreign as it could possibly be to Kevin Phelan, or for that matter most of his family. Nor was he an obvious suspect for an attempt on the lives of his own family. So why were the pair trying to put on a show?

Oddie pushed the heavy armchair round to where he could get a better view of Kevin Phelan behind the table. He sat down and decided not to waste time expressing sympathy. It would be as difficult for Kevin to receive as it would be for him to give. He adopted a businesslike tone short on resonances.

"It's the business of your father's death."

"Aye."

"We're pretty sure that the fire was started deliberately."

"Bastards."

It was said without passion, routinely. Oddie looked at Kevin, curious.

"Whom are you referring to?"

"The bastards who done it."

"Who do you think they would be?"

"Those bastards in Wynton Lane."

"Yes, we . . . got your message about them."

167

An evil smile of self-satisfaction forced its way forward onto Kevin's face.

"The bastards asked for it!"

"Well, we'll say nothing for the moment about the malicious damage aspect of it. What interests me is this: We send a man here in the middle of the night to tell you that your father has died. By daybreak you've announced to the world that one of the people in Wynton Lane did it."

"Well?" More aggressively now.

"You assumed it was deliberate, and you assumed it was one of them who did it."

"People hated my Dad." This was said with real relish.

"Then why assume it was them?"

"He was going to move in there. They'd do anything to stop him. Toffee-nosed gits."

"I still think those are two pretty breathtaking assumptions to make."

Kevin thought. He had trouble with words of over two syllables.

"I told you why."

"Well—let's let that pass for the moment. We gather your Dad had had a win on the football pools."

"That's right."

"A big win?"

"S'pose so."

"You don't know?"

"No."

"That seems odd. Why not?"

"Wouldn't tell me. He bought me a drink at the Railway King, but he wouldn't tell me. Crafty old bugger, me Dad." Once again this was said with relish: Kevin admired craftiness and villainy wherever it was to be found.

"Who would have known how big it was?"

"Me Mam. . . . Maybe me Mam. You never knew wi' me Dad. He could have not told her either."

"But so far as you know your father was intending to buy the house in Wynton Lane?"

" 'Course he was. Been to a s'licitor an' all."

"Yes. . . . Getting back to the night of the fire. Where were you during the evening?"

"Here." It came a fraction too fast and too loud. It was followed up glibly. "Jason and me was both here. Watching the telly. We was skint."

"I see. Any independent confirmation of this?"

"What?"

"Anyone visit you? You talk to anyone?"

"Don't think so? What's it matter? Jason was here wi' me the whole time."

Oddie merely raised his eyebrows. He would soon make it clear, if necessary, how much it mattered.

"So you went to bed—when?"

"About half past ten."

"Right. And you slept until you were woken up by one of our policemen?"

"That's right."

"Then went to find and tell your sister June."

"Yeah."

"How long did that take?"

"We went to Carrock on Jason's motorbike his mother give him for his eighteenth, lucky git."

"How long did it take you to find her?"

"We never did."

"So you went on to Burtle and did your spray job?"

"That's right. Back here and got the spray gun, then out and done it. Bet that set people talking."

His tongue flicked round his lips in pleasure.

"Where had your sister June been that night?"

"I dunno, do I?"

"You didn't ask her?"

"I ain't seen her, have I?"

"What?" The truth struck Oddie suddenly. "You mean she doesn't know about the fire, about her father's death?"

"I dunno. Not as far as I know."

Oddie swore, and turned to Sergeant Stokes.

"We've been bloody fools. Get on to HQ. I want her found, told, and questioned. How could we have forgotten her?" Stokes got up, but they were interrupted by a knock at the door. Jason Mattingley had been lurking in the background during Kevin's questioning, and now he went to open the door. Detective Constable Bramley came in and leaned over to whisper in Oddie's ear.

"There's been a can of petrol in the shed round the back. You can see the outline on the floor, and there are recent spillages that still smell strongly. It's been got rid of."

Oddie sat back in his chair. The room was very quiet. He was being watched by the two boys, who nevertheless were quiet, tense. They had tried to stage this meeting, and it had not worked. He looked at Kevin, sitting on the other side of the table. . . . Why in their staging had Kevin sat *at table*?

Because on the sofa, in the armchairs, he would be too exposed—was that it? What was he trying to hide?

An idea struck him.

"Let me see your hands."

"What?"

"I want to see your hands."

Slowly, his lips tightened, Kevin drew up his hands

from their position under the table. The right hand was puffy, shiny, unnaturally red. At some time, though not recently, Oddie felt sure that that right hand had been badly burned.

"So that's what you've been trying to hide."

"I never tried to hide it. I went to Pickering with it."

"I'm going to have to ask you to come with us—" he began. But only began. Now Kevin had done with play-acting and restraint, and he launched himself on them, abetted by his mate, with a vicious frenzy that made Oddie grateful for his foresight in bringing two other men with him.

It was good to have them behind bars. Both of them behind bars, and separately. Magistrates always took a serious view of assaults on police officers. When they were both on remand he could probably get Jason Mattingley holed up in Apsely Jail with a sympathetic old lag who would give him good advice about shopping a mate who was obviously nothing but bad news.

Even without Jason's help Oddie thought he would be a match for Kevin Phelan, but with Jason he could nail him much more quickly.

When the formalities were over, and with his ears ring-ing with a more concentrated dose of obscenities than even he could remember, Oddie went to his office and found a message waiting for him from the Sleate Infirmary: Mrs. Phelan was through the worst and could be interviewed, though the session would have to be brief and not confrontational. Good. Just the thing, to let Kevin Phelan cool his heels alone for a few hours. He put Sergeant Stokes in charge of the search for June Phelan. "That was a bad mistake we made," he said, "assuming Kevin had got in touch with her. Concentrate on Carrock, then on any of the other red light districts."

Just before setting off an idea hit him. He phoned through to the Chief Superintendent for authorization to use a member of uniformed branch, then got a message through to Malcolm Cray, who was on the beat in the University area to meet him outside the Sleate Infirmary. Having her rescuer in on the interview might help soften Mrs. Phelan's view of the police. Well, it *might*. It was worth trying. Oddie was not too hopeful.

The Infirmary was a warren writ large, a squat pile which had been built in Victorian times and had expanded to meet needs with little regard for architectural niceties, and precious little for convenience either. The corridors were pretty much the same as they had been when Tom Makepeace wheeled patients from the wards to the operating theatres or the mortuary—indeed, they were pretty much as they had been when the old queen was on the throne. Bright new equipment that could do everything except abolish death stood in solid, shabby rooms which told of a Victorian propensity to do good, and to feel good about doing it. Colored lines on the floor in the corridors led you to where you wanted to go, supposing you were in on the secret of the colors. Oddie and Malcolm Cray lost their way twice before they found themselves outside Mary Phelan's room—a single-bed ward, with intensive care. Two nurses, one brown and one white, were fiddling with a collection of bowls and unpleasant-looking probing instruments on a trolley outside the door.

"I've come to talk to Mrs. Phelan," said Oddie in a low voice. "I'm a police officer—it's been arranged."

One of the nurses nodded and pointed to the door.

"How is she mentally?" asked Oddie. The two looked at each other and suppressed giggles.

"It's difficult to say," said the white one.

"*You'll* see," said the other, and they wheeled their trolley away down the corridor, talking in a whisper and giggling.

Mike Oddie raised his eyebrows at Cray and walked in.

Mary Phelan's room was in half light, but her heavy figure could be made out on the bed, more rock than jelly. She was wearing a hospital nightdress, but nothing could have softened the square shoulders, the breasts like boulders on the Icelandic tundra. She was gazing ahead of her—not blankly, but with a kind of purposiveness that did not include her visitors. She made no acknowledgment of their arrival beyond a glance at them as they came through the door.

"Mrs. Phelan? I'm Superintendent Oddie and this is P. C. Cray. You'll know him, of course—your neighbor. It was P. C. Cray who got you out the other night."

He waited. Several seconds of silence.

"Oh, yes?"

He waited again. She added no thanks. Malcolm Cray thought: They're not in her repertoire either. The two men sat down on either side of the bed. Mary Phelan continued to look straight ahead.

"Mrs. Phelan, you probably know that we think the fire was started deliberately. Tell me, do you have a clear memory of the evening before the fire?"

"Yes."

"Will you tell me what happened?"

173

She had obviously realized she was going to be questioned, was used to police questioning. She spoke in short bursts, as if she had other, more important things on her mind.

"Jack was down the King. Kids went to bed about half past nine. I went down to have a light ale with Jack. Come back about quarter past ten. Went straight to bed."

"And you don't remember anything after that?"

"No."

"Did your husband come home with you?"

"No. Mean bugger—he'd only buy me one. Stayed on to have a last one himself."

"Did you hear him come in?"

"No. I was right off. Knew he'd stay downstairs anyway, front of the telly."

"You say your husband wouldn't buy you a second drink, Mrs. Phelan. But he did, in fact, have plenty of money, didn't he?"

Something happened on her face that was not a smile, more like the slow cracking of the rockface.

"Geddaway."

"He didn't?"

" 'Course 'e bloody didn't!"

"But what about the pools win?"

"A hundred and eighty-nine pounds, forty-five pence. We bought a secondhand telly because ours was on the blink, and we got a crate of Tetleys beer and a bottle of whiskey, and we ate well for a week. And that was about it."

"So the suggestion that you were about to buy the house in Wynton Lane was—"

The crack slowly crossed the face again.

"Always did think himself a fucking wag, did our Jack. Now look where it's got him."

"What do you mean? You think one of the people in the Lane started the fire?"

"Well, what do you think? Bloody obvious, i'n't it?"

"Has your son Kevin been to see you in hospital?"

"Bin in and out."

"Did he suggest that?"

"He didn't bloody need to. It's obvious."

"Kevin himself burned his hands some time ago, didn't he?"

"I dunno. . . . You want to lay off our Kevin. Always picking on him, you lot."

It was said without an ounce of conviction or passion—one of the standard Phelan responses to police questioning.

"So you don't know how he burned his hands?"

"No. He's bin moved out months and months now. I'm not responsible for *him* anymore, thank Christ."

"And the idea that your husband had had a big pools win was nothing but a joke?"

" 'Course it was a bleeding joke. Just the sort of thing that tickled our Jack. When we got the win, first thing he did was he got the Estate talking, just by buying a round of drinks. Thought everyone would come buzzing round him like flies, licking his arse in the hope of a handout. But they never did. People were wary of our Jack. He could be right nasty at times. So then he got the idea of going to view the house in the Lane. There's a wet week from the Social Security lives in one of them houses—he come to accuse us once of mistreating our kids. Bloody cheek. He was seen off, I can tell you. *And* there's that bleeding headmistress or whatever she was, that used to come around about our June. Old Lady Nevershit—that's what Jack used to call her. They're a snotty-nosed lot, them that live there."

"But your husband went further, didn't he? He went to see a solicitor."

"He wasn't going to go to a solicitor. He was on his way to a bloody dog-fight, down Barnsley way. But he saw that prick from the Social Security sitting at the back of the bus—saw him in the mirror at the top of the stairs. When he got off he saw him following him, so he went into the solicitor's. Don't reckon the solicitor took Jack all that seriously. Any road, we never heard from him. Just gave Jack a big laugh, to stir it up a bit more . . . Doesn't look as if he had the last laugh, though, does it?"

Oddie didn't see any way of shaking her conviction that the people of Wynton Lane were responsible for the fire. Her son had put the idea into her head, and now nothing would get it out. Maybe she even had some dim idea of screwing compensation out of them. But at least the talk had cleared up one matter.

He stood up.

"The doctor said I wasn't to have more than a quarter of an hour with you. Is there anything else you'd like to tell me?"

"No."

"There's nobody else your husband got on the wrong side of?"

"No. . . . Well, there's one or two. Like I said, folk was wary of him. But them round the Estate's fucking hopeless. There's no way one of them would have done it."

By the door Oddie paused.

"Well, that's about it, for the moment."

But Mary Phelan was leaning forward in her bed, looking at him with an intensity and an interest which the substance of the interview had not aroused.

"Could you do something for me?"

"Well, yes, of course, if—"

"The doctors here are right bastards. Could you fetch me in a couple o' cans of light ale?"

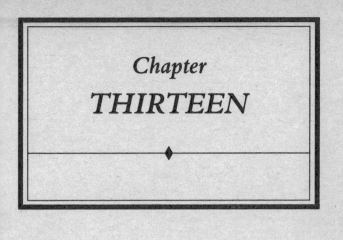

Chapter

THIRTEEN

Michael Phelan went back to school on the Monday after the fire. He was quiet, thoughtful—even a little dreamy. He was still staying, Carol knew, with the Crays, though he had plucked up courage and been round to talk to Mrs. Makepeace. What his emotions had been when he had seen the blackened shell of his former home could only be guessed at. Carol said, "It's good to have you back, Michael. We were all very sorry." He nodded and looked down at his desk. She gave him no special notice for the rest of the morning, though, in fact, she kept an eye on him.

Bob McEvoy was a great help. He had the bright idea of scheduling an impromptu rehearsal for Speech Day in fourth period—the last before dinner break. Carol had the period free, and when she had marked a few books and listened to Dot Fenton ponificating about "children" in the common room, she went along and stood at the back of the gym to watch. Michael was now performing, and in the grip of the words. He had lost that trace of dreaminess and he *was* Growltiger the cat, realizing him bodily as well as verbally.

> *Growltiger was a Bravo Cat, who travelled on a barge:*
> *In fact he was the roughest cat that ever roamed at large.*
> *From Gravesend up to Oxford he pursued his evil aims,*
> *Rejoicing in his title of "The Terror of the Thames."*

This was not a reading but a performance. The thought occurred to Carol as the reading progressed ("Woe to the pampered Pekinese, that faced Growltiger's rage. . . . But most to Cats of foreign race his hatred had been vowed . . .") that some hints for his interpretation could have been gained from a nonfeline creature very close to home. The thought caused her a twinge of embarrassment, but, of course, the poem for recitation had been chosen before his father's death, and it would cause too many problems to change it now. The relish of Michael's performance showed that the idea had not occurred to him. He stayed in character for as long as he went through details with Bob McEvoy—wrong stresses on words, dubious pronunciations, suggested movements at various points. Then—another small miracle—as soon as Bob had finished with him he reverted from actor to boy: Michael Phelan, unusually clean and spruce, but otherwise very much as he had always been.

Carol stayed until the end. This was not just for Michael's sake. There was niggling at the back of her mind the question of whether she just liked Bob McEvoy as a person, or whether—but it is unnecessary to be specific: It was the age-old question, as Carol was well aware, and the success or otherwise of a future marriage would depend on her finding the right answer to it. At the end of the rehearsal Michael came up to her and smiled, very much his old self.

"Was I all right?"

"You were good, very good, Michael."

Together they walked companionably back through the playground to the main school building.

"You're still with Mr. and Mrs. Cray, aren't you, Michael?"

"Yes. They've been smashing. They say I can stay until Mum comes out of hospital and they give us a new house."

"Have the housing people said when that will be?"

"They've told Malcolm they'll find us something. That Mrs. Bridewell has been on to them."

"Your mother will need a lot of support, now that your Dad's not there."

As she said it, Carol realized that this was a cliché that in this case hardly applied.

"I suppose so . . . though in a way it may be better."

"Maybe it will. Anyway, the main thing is that you're getting over it all right."

"I suppose I am. But it was a rotten thing to do. He wasn't much, but he was my Dad."

It was, Carol recognized, a moral judgment, a finely tuned epitaph. Michael was growing up.

When the call from the police came through, Lynn Packard readily agreed to drop everything at Foodwise and talk to them. He had been intending to lunch at the Yuppiehole, a wine bar whose appeal to its intended clientele was as blatant as its overcharging. Lynn had gathered around him a little braying circle there who talked only of money, and then only in "thou's" and "hundred-thou's." But he told Superintendent Oddie that he'd be only too happy to have a chat, though he didn't see how he could help. No—he would come round to Police HQ. Visible policemen were always bad for business, even when a shoplifter had been caught, and they were always shuffled quickly away into the back of the store, like some unpresentable tradesmen. Also, Lynn didn't want anyone at work to know he had been interviewed. Subordinates talked—it was the way they compensated for being subordinate.

He wished he could be more relaxed. He had, after all, pretty much expected to be interviewed by the police ever since he had seen that flaming accusation, which, in spite of Daphne Bridewell's decorator, still shrieked at passersby and brought the blood to his cheeks every time he drove down Wynton Lane. The fact was he had been unable to attain equanimity about the prospect. Only that morning Jennifer had said to him: "You're scared, aren't you?" Bloody Jennifer! She had been very odd lately. Saying a thing like that was hardly the way to bolster his confidence. Lynn believed firmly in the supportive role of wives. In fact, he needed it. Like most people who spoke too loudly, he was very unsure of himself.

So when Mike Oddie had shown him into the interview room, and while his sergeant was fetching him a cup of quite deplorable coffee, Lynn stretched out his feet under the table and smiled with apparent ease at the superintendent on the other side of it, but there was in his stomach an aching emptiness of unease which found its expression in an audible rumble.

"Sorry!" he said. "My usual eating time."

Mike Oddie nodded and smiled.

"Sorry about that. Only time we could fit you in. Well, let's get down to it, shall we? You're probably not surprised at our wanting to talk to you. That accusation sprayed on the wall—"

"That damned vandal!"

Too loud. Lynn knew it as soon as the words were out. Oddie just smiled.

"Ah, yes. Kevin Phelan. You'll be pleased to know that we have him in custody—"

"You have? That's great! I always said this was a gutter crime. Any help I can give—"

"—on another matter. We have arrested him on another matter."

The letdown was immense. It showed in Lynn's face, and Lynn knew that it had shown in his face. Oddie went on:

"We've found nothing yet to connect him with the fire at his old home. But since he's in custody you can get on with wiping off that inscription without being afraid that he'll come back and do it again the next night."

"Oh, yes. Thanks. Actually we've had someone trying to do something, but—"

"They tend to stay visible. Yes, we know. Now, I've talked to Dr. Pickering, so I know what the accusation refers to. Perhaps in your own words you'd like to give me an account of the efforts the Wynton Lane residents made to stop Phelan moving in."

"Ah, yes." Lynn stretched out still farther and, if anything, still more easily. Once again his stomach betrayed him. "Well, this all started with Algy Cartwright. No—I lie: It started with Mrs. Eastlake, an invalid lady in Willow Bank, the house next door to The Hollies. Lived in the Lane practically since the war. Well, she saw Phelan come to The Hollies, with a key, obviously with permission to view, and, though she hadn't talked to anyone but her son for years, so far as I know, she got on the phone to Algy Cartwright. Both elderly people, you see, and understandably nervous. The rest of us felt we really had to do something to help."

"I see," said Mike Oddie, letting no trace of skepticism seep into his voice. He did not doubt the facts of this account so much as the emphasis.

"So we got together a little meeting. To see what could be done. Of course, we had to make it clear to the old people that there wasn't a lot we *could* do—persuasion, warning, and so on—but at least we could try to set their minds a little at rest. So we all of us—the younger ones, mostly—did what we could: spoke to Pickering, the estate agents, the building societies, and so on. Alerting them about the Phelans. That's about it, really. Not much we could do, when it came down to it."

"I see. Where was this meeting held, sir?"

"Er, at my home."

"And were there any further meetings?"

"Well, yes, we did get together after we'd talked to all these people."

"At your house?"

"Er, yes." The memory rang in his ears of his own voice, at the meeting, cleaving through the general hopelessness and depression with: "The best thing you can do with people like that is put them down, like animals." He put the memory from him. He wasn't the only one who'd gone too far. "We got together, pooled our experiences, and so on. We all felt that Pickering had been—well—less than helpful, to put it frankly. We were disappointed in him, as an old neighbor. But we had put people on their guard, made clear what very unreliable customers these Phelans were, so we felt we'd done all we could to calm fears."

"Of the older residents?"

"Exactly."

"You always regarded the threat as a real one?"

"Of course. He'd had a big win on the pools. He even went to a solicitor."

"That's as may be. Solicitors don't see bank balances. You wouldn't get far toward putting a deposit on The Hollies with a pools win of £180-odd."

Once again Lynn's lack of self-control betrayed him: His face said as clearly as anything that the fuss had been for nothing, that he could have saved his efforts.

"Not that it makes any difference, one way or the other," Lynn spluttered at last. "We all found out there was nothing we could do about Phelan."

Mike Oddie decided to state the obvious.

"Someone found something to do about him," he said.

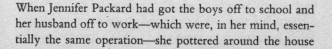

When Jennifer Packard had got the boys off to school and her husband off to work—which were, in her mind, essentially the same operation—she pottered around the house for a bit, but soon landed up at the kitchen table with a cup of coffee and a rare cigarette. She needed to think.

When she had accused Lynn that morning of being scared, she hadn't meant anything more than that he'd got himself so deep into the drive to keep Phelan out of The Hollies that he was now afraid of being accused of setting fire to his house. She was quite sure—almost quite sure—that he had not done so, if only because it did not seem to her that he had the nerve. But watching Lynn in full cry this last couple of weeks or so had certainly hastened the process of seeing him in a new light.

Funny: She remembered a time early in the marriage when she had been desperately afraid he was going to ditch her. She had got the idea that he had mentally stamped a "sell by" date on her bare shoulder—that after three or four years he would find he needed a fresher, younger partner. That was when she had thought of Lynn as a really high flyer. He hadn't, in fact, flown as high as all that, certainly not as high as he had intended. And, beyond a few casual infidelities she could guess at more easily than she could care about, he had never shown any signs of wanting to split up. She had irritated him a lot recently, but he had taken it out on her in his usual way—braying recriminations, assertions of what he "had a right to expect" (a great deal too much, in Jennifer's opinion). A marriage of the sort that they had established over the years obviously suited him.

No, if the question of splitting up ever did come up now, it would be raised by her. She could draw up in her mind a kind of balance sheet. On the one side, there was the fact that Lynn no longer excited her or even pleased her in bed (common enough, no doubt); that she was by now unsure whether she even liked him, let alone loved him; that she was fed up with being an appendage, an automatic support, a nonpersonality hitched to his career. On the other side, there were the boys, who undoubtedly would be unhappy and disorientated if their parents split up; there was the question of where she would go and what she would do (it was so long, so frighteningly long, since she had *done* anything); there was a residual feeling for Lynn that she rather suspected was pity; and there was a terrible doubt in her mind, a feeling that she would be no more happy and fulfilled outside marriage than she was inside it.

She wished she had someone to talk to. Odd all her women friends had somehow fallen away—married, moved, got other interests. Perhaps all domesticated women found this. Or perhaps it was largely her fault: She had been so enthusiastically domestic in those early years, particularly after the births of Gareth and Tristram. She wished she knew better the woman Steven Copperwhite was living with. What was her name? Evie Soames. She looked like the sort one could talk this sort of thing over with.

Margaret Copperwhite realized at once that she had made a big mistake. It had seemed sensible, on consideration, and less painful for her, to invite Steven *out* for a meal, rather than back to the house they had once shared. So easy for him to get the idea that he could treat it as some kind of second home. On no account would she go along with that. She had been twice to the Pot au Feu at lunchtime (once with Mike Oddie, as a matter of fact) and had found it a sensible, streamlined restaurant, catering to busy professional people. She had not realized that in the evening it went in for low, romantic lighting and faint, yearning string music that was probably recycled Mantovani.

"Now this *is* nice," Steven said, showing she'd got it exactly wrong. Quite apart from the fact that it was a damned sight more expensive than a vegetarian nosh-up at the Art Gallery.

"Mmmm," she murmured noncommittally.

"This is a luxury," said Steven when they had ordered. "It's ages since I had dinner out, or—"

He stopped himself in time. He had been going to say "or had dinner cooked for me, come to that." But he didn't want Margaret to think he was whingeing. She doubtless would think he had made his bed, and must lie on it. Might even, indeed, crow.

In spite of his constant attempts at honesty with himself, Steven had never quite admitted what his motives were in resuming relations with his ex-wife. He was hedging his bets. At the back of his mind, he knew that Evie, so much younger than he, might well before long walk out on him. Then he would be alone, and slightly ridiculous. In fact, sometimes he thought he might make the first move himself—something in the nature (though he would never have used so militaristic a metaphor) of a preemptive strike. But these thoughts remained at the back of his mind. Steven's honesty with himself was really part of his desire to think well of himself, and if realities were too brutal they were shunned.

"I hear they've g—" he began, and then stopped himself again.

"I beg your pardon?"

"Sorry. As a matter of fact, I was going to say 'I hear they've got young Phelan, even if it is for something else.' Then I thought you'd probably think I was trying to pump you again. Unfortunate choice of topic."

"No reason why we shouldn't talk about that," said Margaret, who saw no other topic on the horizon. "So long as you don't expect any information I've gleaned from my job."

Steven nodded intelligently.

"I realize now what fools we must have looked," he said, relaxing. "The middle classes, fighting to defend their patch."

"It *did* look rather like that."

"But I still think it's a complete red herring."

"How do you mean?"

"I think that crime has all the hallmarks of a quite different *sort* of criminal. National Front, bullyboys, terror tactics—that's what it bears the hallmarks of. And that's not really our sort of crime at all."

"Not middle-class crime you mean?"

"Well—if you want to put it in class terms, yes. I see it more politically. You know what our generation was like."

"Oh, do I?"

"Of course, you remember. All that marching and demonstrating for causes we believed in. Sit-ins and banner waving. At least in those days idealism and liberalism weren't dirty words."

"And are the people in Wynton Lane demonstrators and banner wavers?"

"No, no—of course not. What I mean is, all of us there

191

are responsible, thinking individuals, and it just isn't the sort of thing any of us would *do*."

"Of course, I don't know any of the individuals involved, apart from you," said Margaret. "And I'd certainly pay you the compliment of saying that I can't see you trying to incinerate an entire family to preserve your life-style intact."

Her hand was lying on the table, and he put his own hand affectionately over it.

"Bless you, dear old Meg."

Fortunately the arrival of the waiter with their wine covered her withdrawal of her hand.

◆

When Adrian Eastlake arrived home from work that evening he found his mother in the kitchen, dressed, and preparing vegetables for dinner. It was something he had half-expected would happen soon, but he could not repress his protests.

"Darling, there's really no need for you to do that."

"Adrian, don't fuss. It's something I want to do. I feel I'm getting better."

Adrian too had seen how things were changing. There had been a stunning picture of the Princess of Wales in a red evening gown, one shoulder bare, in his mother's women's magazine the previous week. It had not been clipped out, and the magazine had been left out for rubbish. From the garden, where he had been clearing up for winter, he had seen his mother in the spare bedroom, going through the wardrobe to which he had long ago consigned all her old day clothes. He had felt a lump in his throat, and had raked vigorously to hide his emotion. Now he said, "You must just do as you want, my darling," and turned to leave the kitchen.

That evening at dinner, which they ate after a small glass of sherry each, his mother said:

"Somehow I am going to have to get some new clothes. Everything I have is impossibly dated."

"Good clothes don't date, darling. And you always had good clothes."

"Well, that's true in a way. But no style lasts forever. And everything smells so musty."

"I could get hold of some mail order catalogs."

"Adrian! Have I ever been the sort of person who buys clothes out of catalogs?"

It was a long time since she had rebuked him with such spirit. In her long illness she had become compliant, accepting.

After dinner they played Scrabble, and she played in her old way, with a will to win, chivvying him if he took too long thinking. She did win, and not because he let her.

"I enjoyed that," she said, standing up. "Now perhaps it *is* time for bed."

"You are sure you're not overdoing things, aren't you, darling?" asked Adrian anxiously, standing to kiss her goodnight. "So many steps forward, all at once."

" 'I am half sick of shadows,' " Rosamund quoted. "That's one of your favorite poems, isn't it? Of course, I shall go my own pace. If I find it's too much I shall ease up."

At the door she paused, wanting to say something, uncertain for the first time that evening.

"Adrian, you said something the other day that at the time I didn't understand . . . something about that man who died. Phelan. Adrian, I had never seen that man in my life before the day when he came round to view The Hollies. Do please get that clear in your mind, Adrian."

That night, in bed, Adrian Eastlake wept a little, and remained long, long hours sleepless. His mother was coming back to life, and he was not rejoicing over it. What kind of person was he, that he should wish her to remain as she had been—invalid, vegetable, cocooned? But he had to admit—to himself only—that he did wish that. He had enjoyed doing everything for her, enjoyed fussing over her, having her to himself. She had been all-in-all to him. As he had been to her.

Now things were changing. Soon she would start going out, perhaps seeing old friends again, going to church, having coffee in town. What was so dreadful about that? Who could be so selfish as to resent that?

But he did. His mother's emergence into life seemed to make all those long years of her retirement and his selfless love little more than a dream. It made all his devotion, his service, his tender care something a little ridiculous, misplaced. In fact, it made everything he had done for her seem futile.

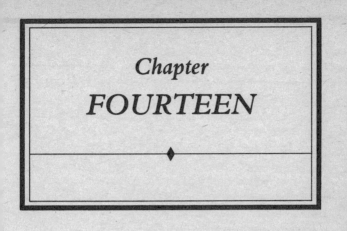

Chapter

FOURTEEN

♦

The girl sat opposite Mike Oddie in the headmaster's study, her eyes knowing, secretive, unwise. The headmaster, sitting unobtrusively beside the desk, had told Oddie that she was a strange girl and, seeing her, he knew that he had an uphill, perhaps an impossible task. The girl licked her lips, which somehow she managed to make an oddly unpleasant motion.

"You're good friends with your sister June, aren't you, Cilla?"

For a moment he thought she was going to deny it—a common Phelan tactic, applied indiscriminately—but at length, without a change of expression, the girl settled for evasion.

"She's my sister."

"That's right, and I expect you talk a lot to each other, don't you?"

She drew a finger across her nose.

"Sometimes."

"You see, we have a problem, because we don't know where your sister is, and we don't even know if she's heard yet that your Dad is dead."

A suspicion of a shrug came into Cilla's shoulders, and she kept silent.

"What I wondered was, is there anyone she's particularly friendly with—a, well, a boyfriend or man friend perhaps? Someone she might be . . . staying with?"

He could have sworn her eyes narrowed slightly, betraying a thought, a name that came into her mind.

"She wouldn't tell me things like that."

She was lying, he knew it. That was just the sort of thing her sister June would tell her. He looked toward the headmaster, whose face was interested but neutral. What sort of tactic, he would have liked to ask, might work with this sort of child? Finding no inspiration in the face— for probably the headmaster was as much at sea with her as himself—he added a touch of majesty-of-the-law to his manner, leaning forward impressively and raising his voice.

"Cilla, I don't think you're being honest with us. It's very silly to hold things back—silly, and maybe dangerous."

He knew at once he had made a mistake. All his own experience of parenthood counted for nothing with this girl. He should have coaxed, not threatened. An expression of obstinacy settled on her face.

"I don't know anything. I don't know where she is."

"I don't think you do. But I do think you've remembered the name of someone, haven't you?"

"No."

"Someone she's fond of, someone she's going with?"

Cilla leaned forward, and for a moment the closed mask on her face slipped and something more direct showed.

"If I did I wouldn't tell you! Fucking cops!"

It was eerie. Mike Oddie knew he had heard the voice of the dead Jack Phelan.

Back at police headquarters, frustrated, and tantalized by the feeling that Cilla Phelan was concealing more than just the name of one of her sister's men friends, Oddie ran into Malcolm Cray, about to start off on a town beat.

"Bloody Phelans," he said. "How are you going on with Michael?"

"Michael? Oh, fine. It's rather odd . . ."

"Oh?"

"He seems to be a nice, normal, well-adjusted boy."

"But?"

"There are no buts. That's what's odd."

"Oh, I see—with that family. Well, I've seen it happen before. A family of absolute crooks and no-hopers and one of them turns out to be a perfectly normal, nice, law-abiding person. Malcolm, do you know if Michael is close to his sister Cilla?"

"I don't know. They're close in age. But it's funny—I don't get the impression he's close to any of them. As if he—I don't know—holds himself aloof."

"Maybe that's part of the process of self-protection. Do you think he could get something out of her?"

"I don't know about that. Isn't she rather a secretive child? That's how she struck me. And remember—they've all been trained to see the police as The Enemy, Michael as well."

"Don't I know it! I've just had a basinful of the unlovely Cilla myself. But this isn't anything criminal. I just want the name of any man June Phelan might be associating with. When I was talking to Cilla I had the distinct impression that she knew a name but wasn't going to let on about it to me."

"I'll do what I can. I'll be off duty by the time school is out. I'll alert Selena and we'll go at it together."

"Mike!"

It was a shout from the doorway. Oddie turned and saw the duty sergeant.

"Are you coming in? There's someone here I think you'll want to talk to."

———————◆———————

"I hear that you've arrested Kevin Phelan."

Mr. Latif was stocky, of medium height, with a rather handsome dark mustache and a worried expression. In normal circumstances, Oddie would have thought him more than a match physically for Kevin Phelan, but, of course, Kevin always saw to it that circumstances were not normal.

"That's right," he said, gesturing toward the other chair in his office. "How did you know? It hasn't been in the local paper."

Mr. Latif spread his hands wide.

"There is a small shop down from his place in Market Street. They saw him and his friend being bundled into a police car. We have a good network."

"Small shopkeepers?"

"That's right. We each have a small area that we serve, so we are not competitors. Often we have family ties too. And we are all, sometimes, threatened. I was asked to come to you because I have better English than most, but I speak for all of us."

"Right. Well, tell me what's been going on. I take it as read, with that boy, that something has been."

Mr. Latif put his hands on his knees and bent forward, his face suffused with urgency.

"What has been going on is intimidation. I have no evidence of anything worse than that, but what has happened is bad enough. What happens is this. They pick on someone—Moslems, Sikhs, members of any of the minorities —anyone who has moved in to a mainly white area, or who owns a shop there. Someone who's feeling a bit insecure anyway. Then the first thing that happens is, during the night they put a lot of rags soaked in petrol through the letter box."

"Ah. . . . When you say they, you mean—?"

"Kevin Phelan and Jason Mattingley. We know their names, you see. We have to inform ourselves, for our own protection. That is the first thing that happens. Then they leave the people alone for a couple of weeks. I tell you, sir, it is very unnerving!"

"You've been one of their victims yourself?"

"Yes, indeed! Then the second time, there are the rags again, and this time there is a note. In my case it said: 'We'll light it next time.' Of course, I am very unhappy about this. I have a young family, a boy and a girl, and we live over the shop."

"Then you're just the sort of people they would choose. What happens next?"

"They come to the shop, the two of them. They come in, stand in front of the counter, and then they take out a box of matches and they light one. Just that. Not to light a cigarette—they just light the match and stand there watching it burn down. They are smiling—that Phelan has a really horrible smile. Then he comes up to the counter and he says: 'I'm skint, mate. Could you lend us fifty?' "

"I see. It's pure extortion. And you paid?"

"As I say, I have a family. I paid."

"You should have come to us."

Latif shrugged.

"Maybe, maybe. Sometimes the police are very helpful to us—sometimes, you understand, not so much. We talked about it, but in the end. . . . After all, what crime had been committed? And if they were put away, they weren't alone. They're members of a party, so-called. If they weren't around, there would be others to take their places. By paying fifty pounds I got peace for several months. There are plenty of small shopkeepers around to frighten, so it is a long time before they get back to me."

"Why have you come to us now?"

Latif smiled, self-depreciatingly.

"Maybe it is easier to do the right thing when your enemy is already in the bag. One of us was at the magistrates' court yesterday, and he said Phelan was up for assaulting a policeman. So his friends will not associate his arrest with us. But if we can get him put away for longer, so much the better. But there is one thing more." He leaned forward, now even more urgent, his eyes fixed on Oddie. "We want you to remember the family that was burned out earlier this year in Armstead. They lived too over their own shop. We think that was a message to all of us: Pay up, or else. We ask you to remember that family."

Oddie nodded.

"We're remembering."

"The police came to talk to Cilla Phelan this morning," said Carol Southgate to Bob McEvoy. It was after school, and they were walking up the hill on their way to Carol's flat and to their first meal together.

"Much good it did them, I imagine."

"No, I can't imagine a stranger getting much out of her, when none of the teachers whom she knows quite well can. She's a strange child—unnerving. That's why I wondered whether she was being abused."

Bob McEvoy nodded. For him it was almost a routine question.

"There have certainly been children in the school who have been—still are: Betty Morton, Mandy Hobbs, for instance. The first shows all the signs, and Mandy's actually with foster parents, who are having a hell of a time with her. But their behavior is open, flagrant. That's not like Cilla Phelan. Hers is the reverse."

"The whisper is the police wanted to know where June might be. She wouldn't even help them with that. I get this feeling all the time that she's *hugging* herself, somehow—over something she knows. And that's not likely to be just where her sister is."

"Something to do with the fire, you mean?"

"Well, it could be, couldn't it?"

"Equally it could be just anything. Children of that age don't have the experience needed to weigh up what they know. She might have seen or heard something that she thinks is wildly interesting and important—and it is, to her. But only to her."

"What sort of thing do you mean?"

"Something silly about someone in her class, for example."

"Maybe. I don't get the impression that that's what Cilla finds interesting." They had turned into the Estate, and were in sight of the burned-out hulk of the Phelans' home. Carol shivered. "She seems such a *knowing* girl. It's not as though her parents would ever have not talked about anything in front of the kids. She seems to have adult curiosity, adult knowledge. I think she would be able to estimate how much a piece of information was worth— how much it could hurt."

Bob McEvoy looked skeptical, and they went the rest of the way in silence.

In the front garden of The Laburnums Daphne Bridewell was bending down, presenting her backside to them. She had found nestling under a hedge a trail of ground elder, her pet hate, and she was spraying it with Tumbleweed through a toilet-roll tube. When she heard the gate, she straightened up.

"Oh, hello, Carol."

Carol was about to introduce Bob to her when she caught directed at him a look of such concentrated disapproval that she just smiled and walked on, down the steps to her basement flat.

Later that evening, after dinner with wine, when they were on the sofa and closer than they had ever been— though not *that* close, for Carol had still not made her decision—Bob said:

"Your landlady didn't like my coming here."

"No, she *didn't*! I saw that. Well, she needn't think I'm going to take any notice. If she disapproves of my having men in the flat, she should have told me when I took it."

"And you wouldn't have, I hope?"

"Of course not. It's none of her business."

"What's she done since she left teaching?"

"Don't ask her that. She's been on the City Council. It

would be like asking Ronald Reagan what he'd been doing since giving up acting."

"What has he been doing since giving up acting?"

"Very funny. She's been active in all sorts of things—parks, the arts, better buildings. She's a bit of a do-gooder, and rather likes the publicity, I think."

"I just wondered whether time had hung heavy. People can get odd fancies when that happens."

"Oh, no, she's been very busy. I've always found her very committed and interested in what I'm doing. I admire her in a lot of ways. She's made a new life for herself after retirement."

After a moment's thought, Bob said:

"Do you remember when I first saw these houses I said I smelled fear?"

"Yes. I've remembered that a lot recently."

"Thinking about it, I suppose middle-class people are always a bit afraid. They have something to lose, but no great power to protect themselves. Maybe having the Estate next door to them, and the Phelans, has just sharpened the fear. . . ."

Later, nestling in the crook of Bob's arm, Carol suddenly started.

"I've just had a thought."

"What?"

"Whenever Mrs. Bridewell thinks of her husband she grimaces. Isn't that funny? Perhaps she does have a thing about men." She giggled. "Odd she should think I ought to share it."

Kevin Phelan had been improved in appearance by his stay in the police cells. They had fetched the most presentable of his clothes from the flatlet, and had forced him to have a bath. Now he sat opposite Oddie in jeans and check shirt and looked almost like a normal, undersized teenager—if you ignored the BLACKS OUT tattoo on his neck, his cropped hair, and his vicious expression. And his language, which now was free of all restraints.

"You're gonna f- - -ing let me out of here, Copper. You got nothing on me. I got mates and if you don't f- - -ing let me go you're gonna be done over so your own mother wouldn't know you."

The language was from bad films, but the voice came out in a low, loaded, vicious stream. Oddie was reminded of a snake—not the big, coily ones the charmers use, but a small, thin, deadly one, that might dart out of the undergrowth at you, kill, and dart back. He sighed.

"Your mates will count themselves lucky if they don't find themselves in here with you. And don't make any mistake: We've got plenty on you. Your disgusting little campaign against the small shopkeepers, for instance."

"Don't know what you're f- - -ing talking about."

"We've got people who will testify to having paid protection money after you've stuffed petrol-soaked rags and threatening notes through their doors."

"They're f- - -ing Paki liars. . . . Anyway you can't get me for a few rags. It was just a f- - -ing joke."

"Don't try and teach me the law, Phelan. We can get you all right. Was that how you got your hand burned?"

"No, it f- - -ing wasn't. It was petrol for Jason's f- - -ing motorbike. I got some on me hands and then I lit a f- - -ing match for a fag and it caught fire."

"Unintelligent even for you. And you went along to the doctor with it, didn't you?"

"Yes, I f- - -ing did."

"Interesting . . ."

He got up and left the interview room, leaving Kevin kicking his heels and swearing, under the eye of a sergeant twice his size. In his office Oddie got on the phone to the main Burtle group practice.

"Could I speak to Dr. Pickering, please? Police here. . . . Oh, Pickering—it's a question about our friend Kevin Phelan. Has he been along to you with a burned hand?"

"Wait a minute. I'll get his file. I put the Phelans' visits out of my mind as quickly as I can. . . . Yes, he came along to the 'sit and wait' surgery. That means he didn't have an appointment but just took his turn and saw whoever was on. It was Evans who saw him, I think, to judge by the handwriting. Was that what you wanted to know?"

"The date. When was this?"

"Let's see . . . damned doctors' handwriting . . . the twentieth of February this year."

"Thank you. Thank you very much."

It was the day after the fire in Armstead in which an Asian woman and her daughter had died.

"How did school go today, Michael?" Malcolm Cray asked that evening over high tea. (How fatherly I sound, he thought. Michael is my preparation for fatherhood.)

"All right. Everybody was very nice. I'm glad I went back. It stops you thinking about it so much."

They were in the dining room of the Crays' postwar semi—a rather spare red-brick house, which they had bought hurriedly when it seemed as if the rise in house prices might drive everything out of their financial reach. Already the furniture was in place in the rooms they had redecorated, and there was a sense of homeliness and order. He and Selena both valued order.

"We're still trying to get in touch with your sister June," he said. "We think she may not know yet about the fire, and your Dad."

"She won't have read it in the papers," said Michael, considering. "She doesn't read them. Maybe someone she's with could have read about it and told her."

"Does she have any special friend?" Selena asked casually.

"I expect she does. . . . She's on the game." Michael looked at them quickly, with a sudden access of shyness, to see how they took it, then he added, "Part of the time, anyway."

"Yes, we did know that," Malcolm said. "Do you know of any special man friend?"

Michael shook his head.

"Do you think your sister Cilla would know?"

"She'd know if anybody would."

"She wouldn't tell Superintendent Oddie when he asked her today."

"She wouldn't. She's silly. She likes . . . knowing things, and not telling people about them. Silly things."

He spoke about her as if she were any girl in his class at school. Malcolm was struck again by the air of detachment he had. It was as if he was in the Phelan family but not of it. He remembered Oddie's remark about self-protection, and wondered whether the detachment was part of Michael's recipe for survival.

"Wouldn't she talk about them even to you?" Selena was asking.

"I don't think so. She might. It would depend what mood she was in, really."

"Do you think you could talk to her? Find out any men—anyone at all—your sister June might be with."

"I could try. I'll go around when I've finished my tea. It'll be a man," he said again, with that air of consideration. "If she's gone a long time it's always with a man."

Later that evening, close to bedtime, he came back triumphant.

"Cilla was going out," he said. "Mrs. Mattingley has been going on at her about visiting Mum in hospital and Cilla wouldn't, made out she hated hospitals, till in the end Mrs. Mattingley had to go along with her—practically dragging her."

"So you talked to her friend," said Selena acutely.

"That's right. Gail. She's silly too, just like Cilla. But she wasn't so on her guard, like. We just talked, and when it got round to June she said Cilla thought she was with somebody called Waley. That's all she knew. Somebody called Waley."

Later that evening, when Michael had gone to bed, Malcolm phoned through to headquarters and left a message for Mike Oddie: somebody called Waley.

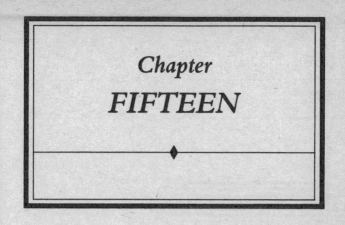

Chapter
FIFTEEN

At ten o'clock next morning Steven Copperwhite stopped toying with a sentence about Muriel Spark which aimed at her lapidary, epigrammatic elegance but kept lapsing into sluggishness and began getting his books together for the day's tutorials. Lawrence and Auden—neither of them favorites of his. He snapped his briefcase shut, wound a West Yorkshire University scarf around his neck, and was just about to go out to the car when he realized he had not heard Evie leave.

He poked his head into the living room and found her at the table, pasting photographs onto a large piece of cardboard. Inevitably, with Evie, he knew that before long there would also be slogans.

"It's the Kirkby Development Scheme," Evie explained, looking up. "There's a protest meeting tonight. What do you think?"

There were two pictures with "Before" and "After" written over them. The "After" was a hideous picture of a shopping complex and a theme park side by side, taken in some luckless city that had suffered those twin contemporary depredations. The "Before" picture was a postcard of *The Hireling Shepherd*.

"They're planning a dinosaur theme park and an enormous Foodwise supermarket with acres of parking," explained Evie. "It's vandalism under the guise of development."

"I know. . . . I think *The Hireling Shepherd* is a mistake."

"Why? I love Pre-Raphaelite pictures."

"Hmmm. They're all right provided you don't see them in bulk. The trouble with this one is there's not the faintest whiff of sheep-dip. The shepherd looks like a public school-boy got up for a rural pageant. Anyway, it's a hell of a long time since Kirkby saw any sheep."

He had her on one of her weak points. Evie came from Essex—the arsehole of England, she called it—and knew nothing of sheep. If a sheep had made an appearance in her part of Essex it would have had a parking ticket slapped on it. She looked uncharacteristically uncertain.

"Something else, then?"

"Yes. And not *Lo, the Pretty Baa-lambs* either. Why not an Atkinson Grimshaw?"

"I'll look for something. You are on our side, though, aren't you?"

"Of course I'm on your side. This government is taking decision making clean out of the hands of the local councils. And their policy on the countryside is absolutely diabolical. England will soon be 'This green and pleasant golf course' if this lot get their way. They'd turn Saddleworth Moor into a Myra Hindley theme park, given half a chance."

"That's very good," said Evie. "I might use that at the meeting." She looked up at him thoughtfully. "But you don't *feel* it, do you?"

"What do you mean? Of course I feel it."

"No, you *believe* it, because it's in line with what you've always believed. And you can coin a good phrase. But you don't *feel* it. Essentially, in your bones, you don't care. Is that because you're getting old, I wonder? Is that what age does to one? Interesting point for your research."

She began collecting her books together for the day.

"You're very unfair," Steven protested. "You really shouldn't say wounding things like that. You give me the feeling that we're splitting apart."

"What nonsense. We were never together," said Evie briskly, rummaging in her bag to find her keys and striding out of the house. At the door she paused. "I think it's great that you're seeing Margaret again."

◆

There were three Waleys in the telephone directory, and one of those was also thrown up by the police computer: William Waley of Waitewood, who had been interviewed at the time of the Carrock child sex scandal—interviewed but not prosecuted. Prosecution had been concentrated on those operating the ring rather than the clients, and even then the police were conscious that the real ringleader had eluded them. With hindsight the clients should probably also have been exposed, but it had seemed at the time that the really important thing was to close down the grubby business. It was at that time, too, that June Phelan had come within the police's ken. They had sent a policewoman to talk to her family. Apparently Jack Phelan's reaction was that it was good she was bringing money in.

"Good thing that the name you got hold of was an unusual one," Mike Oddie said to Malcolm Cray as he passed him in the corridor on his way from the computer room.

"Unusual? Waley?"

"If it had been Walker it would have taken us all week to check. We're in a bit of a rut with surnames in the North."

"Sir," said Malcolm Cray, putting out a hand to detain him. "I had a thought overnight—lying in bed and thinking things over . . . You remember I said just after the fire that he probably knew that some of the family would be away?"

"Yes."

"Well, what if, in fact, it was the other way around? What if it wasn't Jack that was aimed at but one of the children who didn't happen to be there."

"Point taken," said Oddie grimly. "Particularly as I'm on my way, I hope, to interview one of those now."

William Waley lived at number 25, Park View Heights, Waitewood, a suburb where standard red-brick semis slotted in among patches of woodland and school playing fields. Waley's semi was rather superior to most of the other meager specimens—it had a broader frontage, was plastered over and newly repainted, and was probably earlier—thirties rather than postwar. Approaching it casually from where they had left their car, Oddie and Sergeant Stokes saw a good-sized garage, a garden with a few late roses, and a bosomy bay window with heavy velvet curtains pulled across. As they went up the little driveway to the front door, they could hear electronic voices, and through the curtains they caught the flicker of a television screen.

A couple of seconds after Oddie rang the doorbell, the

television was switched off. The house was now totally silent. He rang again. Still only silence. He raised an eyebrow at Sergeant Stokes and bent down to open the letter box.

"Miss Phelan? June? We know you're in there. This is the police. We have some important information for you. Will you open the door please?"

He straightened up. "Seemed worth a try," he mouthed at Stokes. There was still no movement from inside. He sighed and bent himself down to the letter box again.

"Miss Phelan, please listen to me. We have something very important to tell you. If you don't let us in, we shall have to force our way in, so please open the door."

This seemed to work. After a pause of a second or two, there were sounds of scurrying footsteps and the door was opened a few inches. Nothing was said and nobody appeared in the gap, so they edged their way into the house.

"What the hell are you going on about?"

It took them some moments for their eyes to accustom themselves to the gloom of the hallway. No lights were on, and the figure who had opened and quickly shut the door stood behind it in the gloomiest part. She was wearing a brilliant blue dress of a silky material Mike Oddie could not have described, and high-heeled shoes that, like the dress, seemed rather too big for her. She was very heavily made up—indeed Oddie had the impression that she had been experimenting on her face when the doorbell had rung, for one side of the face was made up on rather different principles from the other, and there was a lopsided dash of mascara around the left eye, where the bell had caused the pencil to slip.

"Could we go through?" he asked. "This is important."

There was a shrug of padded blue shoulder and she led

the way. The living room was conventionally furnished, with a heavy padded sofa and chairs, thick fitted carpet, a small bookcase, a large television with video recorder, and a newspaper rack with the local daily paper for the last few days in it. The orderly, middle-class impression of the room was overlaid by another, inimical force: Underclothes and a towel were strewn over the sofa, a mug and a plate were on the television, and a buttery knife had fallen onto the carpet beside it. There was a slum of makeup packs and jars on the mantelpiece, and the contents of them had got over the mirror as well as here and there on surfaces in the room. June Phelan was setting her mark on her space.

"You are June Phelan?"

After a second for thought, she nodded.

"I'm afraid I have bad news for you. There was a fire at your home and your father's dead."

"He's not!" For a moment surprise made her look the sixteen years that she was, underneath the borrowed grown-upness.

"I'm afraid he is. Your mother has been very sick, but she's recovering now in hospital.

"What do you expect me to do?"

It was the automatic Phelan aggression, an indignant repudiation of the world's expectations. The emotion had been surprise, not grief, and she had quickly reverted to the patterns of behavior she had always known.

"That's for you to decide. We just came because we thought you must not have heard the news." He gestured toward the newspaper rack. "It's been in the paper, though."

June shrugged. Papers meant nothing to her.

"The gentleman of the house . . . Mr. Waley . . . he probably read about it."

"Didn't tell me. Cunning old sod."

"You see I have to ask you some questions because I'm afraid the fire that destroyed your house wasn't accidental."

She looked at him with avid, foolish curiosity.

"You mean someone did it deliberate? Someone wanted to fry our Dad?"

"That's roughly what I meant. Maybe tried to kill all of you."

"Christ!" said June. It was an automatic, almost an admiring response, not a shocked one. She did not seriously think anyone had been aiming at her.

"So perhaps we could sit down and I could ask you a few questions?"

She shrugged and pointed at the sofa. They pushed petticoats, tights, and bras up to one end and sat down.

"How long have you been living here, June?"

"What f- - -ing business is it of yours?"

"I'm just trying to find out if whoever started the fire could have thought you would be in the house at the time."

"Don't talk crap. They weren't aiming to get me. Don't you know anything at all about my Dad? Right bloody troublemaker he was. Never happy unless he was stirring it up."

"I know that. . . . Well, how long have you been here?"

"Christ Almighty! . . . About ten days."

"So—" Oddie calculated roughly in his head—"you must have come here not long after you went with your Dad and Mum to view the house in Wynton Lane."

"About three or four days, far as I remember."

"Did your Dad ever tell you how much he'd won on the pools?"

"No." Her face assumed an expression of scorn. "I knew it must be chicken feed."

"How did you know?"

"I knew my Dad. Right bloody joker he was. If he'd really won a tidy sum on the pools he wouldn't have bought a house with it. I tell you, the first thing he'd 'a' done was go out and buy a car. Loved cars, my Dad, and he hadn't had one for ever so many years. Since he'd last had a job. It was the only thing he never managed to get out of Social Security."

"I see. So you've been here since then. How did you come to know Mr. Waley?"

"Oh, I've known him years." She said it airily, as if she were a middle-aged woman, not a teenaged small-time tart.

"But how did you get to know him?"

"Met him, di'n't I?"

"Where?"

"Oh—here and there."

"He's a customer of yours?"

She shrugged. "You could say that if you liked."

"You were involved in the Carrock business three years ago, weren't you? Did you meet him then?"

"May have done."

"Likes little girls, does he?"

She giggled. The subject of men and their sexual habits made her more communicative.

"I take all this off before he comes home. Put on a skinny nightdress, suck me thumb." She perched herself on the arm of her chair and acted it out for them. Neither of them felt greatly aroused. "Silly old bugger. Playing games like that at his age."

She talked of sex—like many prostitutes—as if it were a lot of silly nonsense with which she had nothing to do.

"Has he got a wife?" Oddie asked.

"Had to fly to New Zealand, didn't she? Father died. I moved in soon as the old cat went. Some of her clothes are brilliant, though. Do you think this suits me?"

She was about to get up to parade her slinky finery when the telephone rang. June sank back in her armchair and stayed put.

"I never answer it. He told me not to. It might be her."

Oddie watched her as she waited for it to stop. She exuded something that was not sexuality, merely availability.

"Are you still . . . working in the Carrock area?" he asked when the ringing stopped.

"On and off. When it suits me. Got a girlfriend there with a flat. We use it alternate nights. She goes out with her boyfriend and I take them back there."

"Your customers?"

"Yeah. That was before old Waley with the limp willy got me to come back here. Cost him a packet, it did. . . . Poor old bugger, he's terrified of the neighbors finding out. Tells me I mustn't have the telly on while he's out, mustn't have the radio on, mustn't go out in the garden. F- - - him."

"You must have met a lot of interesting people in your work. Important people."

"May have done." It was said with another shrug. It had been the wrong approach. June was not interested in important people, only in June.

"Anybody spring to mind?"

"We don't talk about the men we go with."

"Professional ethics?"

"Yer what?"

"Never mind. . . . Are they all a bit kinky, like your Mr. Waley?"

"Varies. Some of them like it straight, some of them

like a bit of dressing up, and that. There's plenty like the little girl stuff, but I'm getting a bit past that." She giggled and pushed her breasts forward at them. "I'm a big girl. Old Waley wouldn't be so keen if he could get anybody younger."

"Not so easy now, I suppose, since the police got wise to what was going on in Carrock."

"F- - -ing police! Always poking their bloody noses in! What's it to you how I earn my bloody money?"

It was the voice of the dreadful, dead Jack Phelan again, this time the voice of the right-of-Thatcher libertarian. Oddie didn't pursue the argument.

"We never got who was really behind the Carrock business, did we?"

June was not to be caught like that. She smiled unappetizingly and said nothing.

"How did you come to get in with that game?"

"Friend at school. Said there was money to be made out of these old kinks. . . . Didn't even know the word then. Innocent, warn't I? . . . Anyway I was interested so she took me along, and—well, that was that."

"Who was the friend?"

"Mind yer own business."

"And what sort of thing did you do?"

"What the f- - - do you think I did? Had sex with men. Want me to spell it out? They put their—"

"Didn't your Mum or Dad try to stop you?"

"They didn't bloody know, did they? Wouldn't have done much if they had. My Dad never stopped me doing anything in his life, 'cept if it was annoying him."

"And this went on until we stepped in?"

"Bloody filth! What's it to you? You should have seen my Dad with that policewoman who came round, though. She practically went purple."

"And you've been on the game again—how long?"

"Since I left school. Since July. I must have been off my rocker, giving it to boys for free."

"So recently you've been sometimes at home and sometimes—well, at Carrock and around, on the game?"

June nodded.

"So anyone who did this to your home couldn't have expected that you'd be inside?"

"You're bleeding daft, you know that? There's no one'd want to get me. Think of all those bloody backs my Dad put up, and then you say they weren't out to get him at all. No wonder it took you years to catch the f- - -ing Yorkshire Ripper!"

She was stopped short by a sound. There was a key being put in the front door. Her eyes widened into something like a genuine emotion: fear. Oddie jumped up and darted out into the hall.

"What's going on? I rang from the station—"

It was a smart, tough-looking woman, weary and travel-stained. As Oddie went toward her she caught a flash of blue from inside the living room.

"Oh, I get it. He's been up to his tricks again, has he? And in my bloody clothes—I'll teach you, you—"

She charged in, and for the next five minutes Oddie and Stokes were busy practicing the techniques learned long ago in their uniform days—the techniques for breaking up a "domestic."

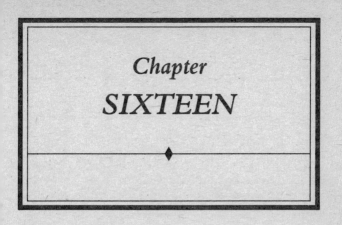

Chapter

SIXTEEN

*S*ince Algy Cartwright had become a widower he had fetched his newspaper each morning from the newsagent's on the other side of the Belfield Grove Estate. This gave to his mornings an element of choice (though he always did choose to get his newspaper, for otherwise what would he read?) as well as a ten-minute walk. So on the morning when Mike Oddie finally caught up with June Phelan, Algy, after a breakfast of poached eggs—which had failed to solve the problem of why, when they looked right, they always turned out to be nearly solid—fetched his copy of the *Daily Express* and walked back past the blackened Phelan house and down the slope toward Wynton Lane.

He spotted her at once, the Jehovah's Witness. Well— Peculiar Person, Mormon, British Israelite, one of those. Algy hated all kinds of canvasser. Badgerers, he called them. He seldom swore, but people who phoned to ask whether he had thought of double-glazing were told to piss off, and canvassers from political parties were told in no uncertain terms that the ballot was supposed to be secret. Religious badgerers were in his opinion the worst of all, for there was no certain way of getting rid of them. Algy's usual tactic of telling them he was a Roman Catholic had once unleashed a passionate diatribe against the Pope as Anti-Christ.

This religious canvasser—her drab clothes and earnest, intense expression gave her away, as well as her handful of leaflets—was being dealt with firmly but politely by Daphne Bridewell. Algy skulked past them to Rosetree Cottage, locked the door, turned off the lights, and retreated upstairs. He went into the spare bedroom from which he had watched the Phelans leaving after their visit to The Hollies and watched the progress of the proselytizer. He had done a lot of watching from that window since the Phelan visitation, a lot of watching and wondering. The murder had certainly given a zest to his drab existence. Mrs. Packard was very short with the woman, ten seconds maybe from door opening to door closing. Evie Soames—she came out of the door, so he could see her—took longer: Perhaps she was doing a bit of proselytizing of her own. Algy had her down in his mind as a good-cause lady. The two had a conversation lasting all of three minutes. Mrs. Eastlake (Algy couldn't see her, but he had seen Adrian go off to work) did open the door, but, like Mrs. Packard, she was brief and decisive. Lovers of the Royal Family tended to be Anglican in sympathy if not in attendance. Nobody much, after all, was Anglican in attendence.

Then the woman went next door to The Hollies. Dr. Pickering had left old curtains up in the windows of the house, to suggest occupancy and discourage squatters. The canvasser went up to the door, rang the bell, then rang again. Algy could see her skirt and legs from beneath the overhanging lintel above the door. After the second ring she disappeared, doubtless down the steps to the basement flat.

Something stirred in Algy's mind. Something Mrs. Eastlake had said when she had first rung him that day of the Phelan visit . . . What was it? . . . The woman had emerged now and was going down to the gate, Christian fortitude in disappointment visible in the set of her shoulders. Algy retreated from his window and went out onto the darkened landing. His doorbell rang, then after a few seconds rang again. A conscientious seeker of souls, this one. A few moments later, he heard the doorbell ring in the basement flat. She wouldn't find *him* in, not his graceless tenant. Out reading gas meters. Cautiously he went back into the bedroom and watched the canvasser retrace her steps, then go up the slope toward the Belfield Grove Estate. Perhaps she would find more fertile ground there. Algy went downstairs, his mind still working, and put on the kettle for a cup of Nescafé.

When the cup was half drunk he went into his hall and got on the phone to Rosamund Eastlake.

"Mrs. Eastlake? Sorry to bother you. It's Algy Cartwright."

"Oh, Algy. No bother."

The voice sounded quite normal now, just like any other housewife. As if she had never withdrawn from the world.

"You'll probably think this is a bit odd, but I've been thinking things over—in connection with this murder, like."

"I'm sure we all have. I would like to see the thing over and done with, for Adrian's sake."

But you've enjoyed it, too, Algy thought.

"Yes, well, I was remembering what you told me on the phone that first time when you rang—about what you saw when the little girl came on in advance of the family. Can you remember? Could you go over it again?"

She could. When she finished Algy said:

"Look, could we try an experiment? I'm going to go next door to The Hollies. I'll stand in the porch and ring on the doorbell. Then I'll go downstairs to the basement. Will you stand at your window, as you did that day, and tell me what you see?"

Five minutes later, having rung on the doorbell of The Hollies and gone down the steps to the basement flat, which was in darkness, Algy was back in his house and on the phone again.

"Now Mrs. Eastlake, Rosamund, what did you see? Did you see me all the time I was on the doorstep of The Hollies?"

"Yes, I could see your legs the whole time. Then you disappeared when you went down to the flat."

"Just like the little girl."

"Yes. But why should that be so significant?"

"Probably it's not. But I was talking to Daphne Bridewell yesterday, and apparently according to that young teacher she's got in her basement flat that Phelan girl is hugging some secret to herself at the moment. And I've been watching a lot recently—"

"Oh, so have I, Algy!"

"—and I've seen that Mrs. Hobbs from the basement flat . . . Well, I won't go into what I saw. . . . I wonder, Mrs. Eastlake, if I were to get on to the police—I know it's a lot to ask—would you be willing to talk to them?"

There was no more than a second's hesitation.

"Of course, Algy. I'm all *right* now. I'm coming round."

When he had talked to Mike Oddie at the police head-quarters, Algy Cartwright on an impulse got on to Lynn Packard at Foodwise in town and told him what he had done.

"You bloody fool!" Lynn brayed. "That brings it back to us!"

"Not really. If I'm right it would bring it back to Mrs. Hobbs."

"Well, maybe," conceded Lynn. "I suppose that's true."

But he didn't have the grace to apologize for swearing at him.

Mike Oddie had taken Algy's phone call soon after his return from the house in Park View Heights. He had a minor cut and a spectacular scratch across his cheek, and he was far from happy. At first he had been unimpressed by Algy, who had been nervous and long in coming to the point. Just another busybody neighbor, he had said to himself. But he had struck gold as well as dross with busybody neighbors in the past, and he had listened on. By the end he was half-convinced that the man just might have a point. At the very least, it was something that was worth checking.

Five minutes on the police computer left him cursing himself for his slackness. He collected Sergeant Stokes from the canteen and together they drove to the houses in Wynton Lane.

When Rosamund Eastlake opened the door of Willow Bank he was immediately struck by her fragile charm. Her dress was too large and faintly musty, but she moved beautifully and her face had the remains of what could only be described as loveliness. Rosamund was the kind of older person for whom the word "policeman" suggests security, comfort in distress. She took to Mike Oddie at once, and instinctively made him feel protective.

"Do come in, Inspector. Is it Inspector? Oh dear, what have you done to your face?"

"Superintendent." Oddie grinned. "The curse of the Phelans, I'm afraid."

"That dreadful family. It's about time we heard the last of them. I have the kettle on for tea."

She led them through to a sitting room that was clean and airy, yet somehow had an underused air, as if any human habitation it had had in the last few years had sat lightly on it. While Mrs. Eastlake went back into the kitchen to busy herself with the tea, Oddie wandered around the room looking at the books in the glass-fronted case, and at the records by the rather elderly record player. Housman, Swinburne, Mahler, Richard Strauss. Romanticism in decay, swoonings toward death. . . . On the other hand, there was Wisden, and the ghosted autobiographies of cricketers.

He bustled to help Mrs. Eastlake as she came in with the tray, and as they settled themselves down he gestured to Sergeant Stokes to take a seat slightly back. Mrs. Eastlake, he could see, was shy, or at any rate nervous: best if she could concentrate on him and forget there was a second man in the room.

"I hope everything is all right," she said, faintly distracted, and gazing at the tray. "It's so long since I've had visitors."

"You've been ill?" Mike's voice was warm and concerned. She responded to it at once.

"Yes. And for so long. . . . Though I sometimes think, now I'm coming out of it, that I've been not so much ill as weak."

"You . . . had a nasty experience, people say."

Mike Oddie had done his homework on the people in Wynton Lane, though he had not found out anything concrete enough to justify interviewing all of them.

"Yes. Best not to talk about that. But I'm beginning to wonder if I didn't—"

"Imagine it?"

"Oh, no, no. I didn't imagine it. But whether I didn't . . . seize on it in some way."

"As an excuse to—what? To give up the world?"

"Something like that. Give up the struggle." She poured the tea and handed it round, then proffered the plate of biscuits. She did not drink the tea herself, but seemed to warm her hands at the side of her cup. "My husband, Desmond, died very young, you see. He was never completely well after the war. We had been very happy—so happy—and quite suddenly, it seemed—because he had hidden things from me, his state of health, what the doctors said—quite suddenly he faded and died. And I was on my own with Adrian."

"Was it a financial struggle?"

"Not really. We've always had just sufficient coming in—Desmond saw to that. But I'd never been the one to take the lead, take decisions. That had been for Desmond to do, and I'd been quite happy to have it like that. I suppose I'm naturally the type who likes to be led. Or perhaps it's a sort of laziness. Then suddenly, on top of the grief, there was this great burden: responsibilities, decisions."

"How old was your boy?"

"Seven. Just seven. And I had to be father as well as

mother to him. Of course, I'd always *loved* Adrian, but somehow—I suppose this sounds dreadful—my life had always centered around Desmond. Then suddenly the center was gone and I had to devote myself entirely to Adrian: give the lead, take decisions, make him look up to me, have confidence in me, as he had had in Desmond. It seemed so *wrong*: What the boy needed was a father."

"I'm sure you did it very well."

"Perhaps. Well enough. He's a dear boy, and very loving. But when he was grown up and had got this job with the Social Security office, which a friend of Desmond's got for him, because poor Adrian didn't have many qualifications —it's been a grief to me that he never had his father's brains, or his looks—when he was settled at last I remember feeling a great wave of relief, and tiredness. Do you understand what I mean?"

"I think so. You'd done your job."

She smiled gratefully. She liked confident men who understood her and sympathized with her.

"That's it! That was it entirely. I felt: Now I can relax, now I can shrug off the burden."

"And then you had your . . . nasty experience."

"Yes." She looked down again, into her tea cup, which was still nearly full. "Yes, it was when Adrian was about twenty-two."

"What was it, Mrs. Eastlake?"

"It's not relevant, nothing to do with anything."

"I don't suppose it is, but it just may be."

She shook her head, her face puckered up.

"I've never told anyone. I don't think I can."

"Was it so horrible?"

"Yes. . . . No. . . . Well, I was frightened . . . disgusted. But it was also . . . almost ridiculous. I was so ignorant, so naive. . . . I didn't know anything about things like that."

"You will feel better if you tell me, Mrs. Eastlake. I assure you I know a lot about people who have had horrific experiences, and they really do feel better for telling someone, getting it off their chests."

She looked up at him glancingly—a shy, timid look that seemed to say "Do you promise?" with the trustingness of a child. Then she looked back into her cup, and there was a long pause before she spoke again.

"It had been a lovely summer's day, I remember, and we had been out in the garden—sitting under the cherry tree, eating strawberries and cream. A perfect day, as perfect as any I'd had since Desmond died. I remember I was wearing my favorite summer dress, very light and gauzy, and I felt so perfectly relaxed. I didn't notice, not consciously, that Daphne wasn't so relaxed . . . was very tense and twitchy. She had been so good to me and Adrian after Desmond died. Not that Adrian went to her school, of course—he was educated privately—but she was so good about helping him with his schoolwork, getting him to make a decision about what he wanted to do. Of course, I'm speaking about a time some years after her husband left her. I never really knew him, only to wave and say 'Good Morning' to, but I had the impression that she was rather glad when he left her."

She came to a stop. Mike Oddie sat quite still—a sturdy, encouraging presence, not breaking the silence with a question. Eventually in a smaller voice she went on.

"A little cloud came over the sun, and there was a slight chill in the air. We thought it was time to go in, and we took the cups and the strawberry bowls into the kitchen. I remember standing at the sink, piling up the crockery. . . .

I remember, like a snapshot, the garden—how lush it was, very green, and the roses—the King's Ransom that Desmond had planted. When suddenly I felt arms round me, fondling me, fondling my . . . breasts, and Daphne telling me she loved me, adored me, and I saw her face in the little mirror by the kitchen window, and it was . . . *avid*. I was so frightened, nauseated, I said 'Please! Please stop! and tried to get away, and she clung to me and pleaded with me, and . . . It went on and on, like a nightmare, something I wanted to wake from and couldn't, and I tried to shake her off, as if she were an animal, and she clung on, and suddenly the front doorbell rang, and I screamed and she ran away sobbing out of the back door."

She came to a halt.

"What did you do?" Oddie asked quietly.

"I remember sinking to the floor, retching. I was frightened and disgusted and—and I just didn't understand. I remember crawling over to lock the back door, crawling through into here. That's how Adrian found me when he got home from work—crying, hysterical, my dress torn, really in a frightful state. . . . He put me to bed. I couldn't explain. I—can you understand this?—I knew nothing about things like that. The thought of . . . unnatural love like that simply never entered my head. I suppose I was an innocent. Desmond had shielded me. Those were different times. It was not the sort of thing we would think of ever mentioning between ourselves. Can you understand that?"

She looked up at him, beautiful, vulnerable, appealing. Mike Oddie murmured, "Of course."

"So you see I couldn't explain. I think he came to believe. . . . Anyway, he was so sweet and kind, and did everything for me, nursed me, mothered me, in a way. And I came to—to like it, rely on it."

"You sort of relaxed into it, after years of taking decisions?"

"Yes, that's it exactly. Like relaxing into a big, comfy chair." She smiled her thanks for his understanding. "And Adrian seemed so to love doing things for me. Nothing was ever too much trouble. He never complained, never seemed to want any other kind of life. Looking back, maybe I should blame myself, but I do think that in his way he has been happy."

She shot him that same look, and he nodded.

"There," he said, "now you've told someone. Does it feel better?"

"Not now. I think perhaps it will. I feel stronger, in a way. As if I had faced up to it a little." She looked at him with a tiny trace of the coquette in her eyes. "Why did I tell you that? It wasn't even what you came to ask about."

"Policemen get used to hearing things," said Oddie, smiling back. "We don't always bully it out of people, as some try to make out. I suppose we develop listening techniques. Yes—what I wanted to talk about was the day the Phelans came to view The Hollies. I gather from Mr. Cartwright that one of them came on in advance?"

"That's right. A little girl—well, one of about twelve or thirteen."

"Cilla," said Mike Oddie with a sigh. "A girl it seems impossible to get anything out of."

"She was the one I saw first. She came through the gate and stood at the front door. I could see her skirt—a revolting purple skirt. Then she disappeared. Of course, she could have flattened herself against the door for some reason or other. But Algy and I tried an experiment, and we think she went down the steps to the basement flat. In each of these houses the part with the flat is set back a bit from the rest, and the steps down go from just by the front door.''

"Yes, I saw that."

"Of course, it may have no significance at all. Children are naturally curious, and you say this one is a secretive little girl. She may just have gone down to look, and then come up again.''

"How long was the time when you couldn't see her?"

She thought, trying hard to help him, wanting to please him.

"Oh—so hard to say after this time. A little while. I mean, not a matter of a few seconds. A minute or more.''

"Do you know the woman in the basement flat of The Hollies?"

"Oh, dear, no. I only know the people who've been here a long time—since before I . . . withdrew myself. Just Algy and . . . Daphne, really. I gather this woman in the flat has only been there a few months. I don't know her at all."

"We do," said Oddie grimly, standing up. "We know Mrs. Hobbs from way back."

They thanked Rosamund Eastlake and made their way to the front door. Mike Oddie congratulated her on confronting the horror in her past, and assured her she would feel better for it, though as they said goodbye it struck him that she was already quite indistinguishable from any other middle-aged woman of great charm and with a strong sense of self-preservation. He and Stokes waved, and then went next door to The Hollies. They took the steps down to the basement flat, but it was darkened, and there was no response to their rings. They had expected as much from Algy Cartwright's account.

"Perhaps it's just as well," said Oddie, back in the car.

"I think it might be best if I did a bit of homework on Mrs. Hobbs before I speak to her."

On the way back to police headquarters, Sergeant Stokes said:

"She seemed a nice woman, that Mrs. Eastlake. Odd story, but charming woman."

"Ye-es."

"You don't agree, sir?"

"I certainly agree she's very charming. Also that she knows how to use her charm, whether she's conscious of that or not. Somebody said that in any love affair there's one who loves and one who consents to be loved. I think Mrs. Eastlake consents to be loved—has done it all these last years with her son."

"You think she's selfish?"

"Self-absorbed, anyway."

"But at least it all seems to have a happy ending, sir. She's coming out of seclusion. The son will be liberated."

"Liberated into what, after all these years when his life has revolved around her? Nothingness, I suspect. But I shouldn't be too harsh. There are worse kinds of love. I'm going to be looking into one of them now."

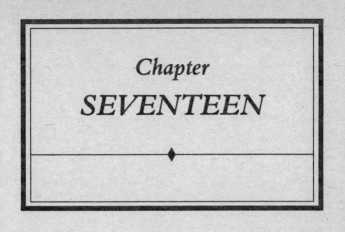

Chapter
SEVENTEEN

♦

*M*rs. Valerie Hobbs arrived back at her basement flat at about ten past four. Mike Oddie heard this not from any plainclothesman left on watch (any such would be conspicuous in Wynton Lane, which contained only those six houses, and led nowhere), but from Algy Cartwright on the phone. They had not asked him to keep watch, but he had kept watch.

"The KGB of Suburbia strikes again," said Mike Oddie to Stokes. "Who needs Neighborhood Watch? We'll give her half an hour to settle down."

When they drove up it was five o'clock, and they left the car some doors away, outside Daphne Bridewell's, though from Mrs. Hobbs's flat, they guessed, there was no sort of view of the road. As they drew up they took in the painted accusation on Daphne Bridewell's wall, now fainter but still easily legible. The residents would only be saved from embarrassment by a much more ruthless treatment, or by an arrest. They walked casually to the flat, through an overgrown front garden and down the steps. From the flat itself, as they stood momentarily outside before ringing, there came the sound of music—Radio One—but not voices. Then they rang the bell.

"Yes?"

The woman who opened the door had a practiced social smile. She was wearing a cardigan, that guarantor of respectability. It was a close machine-knitted affair in pink, above a russet-colored skirt and a blouse with a small, decorous frill running down the length of it. She had a capable, attractive body, a carefully made-up face, and the image created was of one who could organize tea at a Women's Institute meeting or man the Save the Children shop single-handed. As no doubt she could.

"Mrs. Hobbs? We're police officers."

She glanced briefly at their identification to hide her eyes, then flashed at them her five-carat smile.

"Oh, yes. Is it that nasty business on the Estate? The house fire? I saw that dreadful slogan on the wall. Would you care to come in?"

The accent was neutral middle-class but practiced, like her smile, and it had an underlay of something less socially acceptable, something that would have prevented her from ever gaining employment with the BBC. She led the way down a poky passage that led to a dark staircase up to the main part of the house. They, however, turned aside into a brightly lit sitting-room-cum-kitchen. It was furnished with assorted sofas and chairs, secondhand furniture-shop stuff, though the general effect was not really seedy. Trouble had been taken, though not much money had been spent. There was no sign of cooking around the little sink and stove, which stood under a high window that gave out onto the back garden and the lane. Mrs. Hobbs lowered the lighting, which was unflattering, and gestured them toward the chairs.

"Not much room, I'm afraid. I'll be getting out of here soon, when I've found a place of my own."

"Did you know the Phelan family?" began Mike casually.

"The Phelan—? Oh, that's the family whose house was burned down, is it? No, not that I recall. Of course, it's not an uncommon name—Irish, isn't it? And I meet a lot of people. . . ."

Talking too much, thought Mike. Nervous . . .

"I thought you might have met them through your daughter—"

"Oh—well—"

"—your daughter who is in care."

Her lips tautened immediately, and Oddie saw that behind the social smile there was a tight, mean mouth.

"That was totally unfair. The Welfare Services people were quite out of order. I've got my lawyer onto it, but you know how long anything like that takes."

Mike Oddie raised his eyebrows and shifted in his seat, still watching her closely.

"Mrs. Hobbs, let's not beat about the bush. It wasn't just the Welfare Services people who were involved in that matter, it was the police as well."

"You lot can make a mistake as well as them, can't you? It was downright defamation of character."

"It was a question of belatedly protecting a young child. Your daughter was involved in the Carrock child prostitution racket, and so was June Phelan."

"She wasn't taken into care, though, was she? Tell me why that was? Look at the sort of family she has, and then look at the home I was providing for my little girl."

"Ah, so you do know them." Oddie gave a grim smile of satisfaction and it was her turn to shift in her chair. "Now, I've been looking at the notes on that case. June Phelan was only caught up in it just before we swooped—a matter of weeks, no more. Her involvement was marginal, and she was thirteen going on fourteen at the time. Your daughter had been deeply involved for some time, she was eleven—*eleven,* Mrs. Hobbs—and she was seriously disturbed. Still, I gather, is."

She shot him a poisonous look.

"We were a one-parent family. You can't give a child the sort of twenty-four-hours-a-day mothering these days like they used to in the past."

"Come off it," said Mike, letting his dislike briefly show through. "You had no paid job at the time. Your position was hardly different from any other mother's."

"Men!" she spat out viciously. "You think we ought to be chained to the kitchen sink every hour of the day, don't you?"

"We took the view at the time," Oddie went on, ignoring her, "that since Mandy, your daughter, had been involved for some time—over a year, we were sure—and had been getting more and more unmanageable, so that they were seriously worried at Burtle Middle School, where she went—we took the view that there must have been gross negligence, to say the least, on your part. It never occurred to us that there might be anything worse than that."

"Why should it? What are you trying to land on me now?"

"I think the investigating officer assumed, since you

were living comfortably, that you were getting good alimony payments from your ex-husband. But I've made some inquiries of your ex-neighbors. There never was any husband, was there? Nor, as far as we can see, was there any maintenance order against the father of your child."

"Well, what of it? Are you still living in the nineteenth century or something?"

"Not at all. But the question arises, doesn't it, Mrs. Hobbs: How come you were living so comfortably?"

———————◆———————

"It's taken me a while to realize, to sort things out in my mind." Steven Copperwhite was watching his ex-wife as he said it. She gave no sign of a reaction, merely sipped her glass of red wine. He had collected her from work, and they had gone to the Saddle of Mutton in Head Street, which was newly tarted-up Victorian, but quite warm and cozy. He had weighed in with the topic almost at once. "I suppose pride is involved, isn't it? I think underneath I realized my mistake early on. I expect a lot of people who go into second . . . relationships do. What takes the time is acknowledging it to yourself."

Margaret nodded neutrally.

"I mean, the fact is we're miles apart mentally. Evie is so totally committed—really committed, no question of that. But—I don't know—I find I'm too old or too tired for that sort of all-round commitment. I haven't got the fire, the energy. These days I take it easier."

So you want to come back to me as someone you can take it easier with, Margaret thought. She said:

"Of course, one does slow down, at our age."

"Yes. And you start asking yourself: All this activism and commitment—where does it get you, what good does it ever do? Evie seems like a throwback to the sixties. Remember when we used to laugh at Feiffer and Peanuts, and sing 'Little Boxes'? And where did it all get us? A decade of Thatcher and the market as God. No, I realize now that Evie and I were never close. It was an illusion. And we're getting further and further apart all the time. Another red wine?"

Margaret nodded. It would give her time to think.

"The fact is, I made a mistake," said Steven, coming back with two glasses. "I'm not too proud to acknowledge it. I thought it was a great love, a consuming passion, but it was one of those purely physical things."

"Itchy prick?" suggested Margaret.

"Well . . . I suppose so." He threw her a glance and laughed uneasily. "You've changed, Meg. I don't think you'd have used an expression like that when we were married."

"I suppose not. Working in a male environment you pick up the language. Policemen lead pretty dangerous, unpleasant lives these days. They don't mince their words. And, of course, there are plenty of men in the Force who are going through that phase."

"Are there? Yes, I suppose I was suffering from a pretty universal malady. But it *is* only a temporary thing, Meg. I don't know what causes it—fantasy, vanity, all sorts of things you can't disentangle. But I do know now that I made a fool of myself, and I do know that I've come through it."

Margaret nodded slowly.

"Meg, I'm going to ask you to do a big, brave thing."

"Yes," she said.

"Let me move back. I know things can never be quite the same—I'm not such a fool as to think they can—but there's no reason why they shouldn't be pretty good. We really jogged along very pleasantly in the past, didn't we? I won't mention the children, because they're grown up and moved away now, but they *would* be happy if we got together again."

"What about Evie?"

"She wouldn't suffer. The house is in both our names. I'd just let her have my share. I'd leave the furniture. It's not much anyway. I could get together my things quite easily—clothes and books is really all it amounts to. It *would* work this time, Meg dear. I know what a fool I've been. I'd sweat to make sure it worked. Please say yes. I could just pile my things into the car and be with you tomorrow night."

She looked ahead of her, expressionless, thinking. Then silently she dipped her hand into her handbag, took out a key, and handed it over the table to him.

"Sometimes I think Lynn is going off his head," said Jennifer Packard.

She had come next door with the usual housewife's excuse of wanting to borrow something. She had intended to ask for baking powder, but one look at the kitchen of Ashdene had convinced her that little baking was likely to go on there. She had compromised on sugar. The sugar Evie rustled up was raw, but it had served its purpose of providing the opening for a heart-to-heart.

"You don't mean you think he's involved in all this?"

"Oh no, I'm sure he's not . . . Quite sure. . . . But he can't get away from the fact that he masterminded all the opposition to the Phelans, and he knows the police are interested in him just for that reason."

"So the old line about 'If you are innocent you have nothing to fear' doesn't cut any ice with him? I would have thought he'd be a member of the Aren't Our Policemen Wonderful brigade."

"He is, normally. Though he's also fond of watching Sylvester Stallone dispensing his own brand of justice—pretends he's hired them for the kids. I think the mere fact that the police are interested in him makes him feel that his respectability is threatened. He's very insecure socially."

"Aren't we all? Steven thinks my mother is an upper-class dragon, but she's only precariously upper-middle. It's the precariousness that makes her a dragon. She made sure she caught an elderly knight for a husband, and now she waves the title and puts it on generally to an embarrassing extent."

"Yes—I suppose anyone who has anything to lose is socially insecure," said Jennifer thoughtfully.

"That's what makes the Phelans frightening. They have nothing. Jack Phelan was the new underclass: riotous, savage, with nothing to lose. It frees you from an awful lot of restraints and inhibitions. Like the man in *Little Dorrit* who said that being in the debtors' prison gave him freedom, because it was the bottom, and he couldn't fall any further. What are your feelings about your husband?"

"I don't know altogether. I was thinking the other day how I not only didn't love him anymore—that must be common, almost the norm—but I don't even think I like him. I've seen through him, realized there isn't anything much there."

"I know the feeling. Why don't you leave him?"

"The boys, I suppose. It would upset them if we split up, and they're just the wrong age to face disruption of that kind. Lynn is an awfully nagging kind of father, but in his way he's fond of them. Then I wonder how I could possibly manage—finding a home for us, getting a job."

"You don't have to find a home. These days the wife gets the man out."

"Well, I'd have to get some kind of a job, that's for sure. And I genuinely don't think it's good for children not to have a parent home in an emergency . . ."

She trailed off uncertainly.

"There's something else, isn't there?"

"Well . . ." Jennifer screwed up her face in self-dissatisfaction. "I do worry about Lynn. If he shows signs of cracking up now, what's going to happen to him if we all up and leave? It's almost as if he won't exist if he doesn't have us. He seems just a shell of a man. . . . I suppose what it comes down to is I *do* feel something for him, and that's pity."

"That's what most women feel for their husbands after a time," said Evie briskly. "That's why I shall make damned sure I never have a long-lasting relationship."

"Well?" said Oddie.

"Well what?"

She had been gazing stubbornly ahead of her, blank as a wall, and saying nothing at all.

"How did it come about that you were maintaining a comfortable life-style a couple of years ago when you were not receiving alimony or maintenance for Mandy, your daughter, nor did you have a regular job?"

"Mind your own bleeding business."

The mask of the upwardly mobile independent woman was beginning to slip badly, and so was the accent. Oddie realized that she had been running her business for years without ever coming into serious conflict with the police. It reflected very poorly on himself and his colleagues.

"Another very interesting question: Why did this comfortable life-style I've mentioned begin to collapse about the time we closed in on the Carrock business, bringing you down to this?" He waved his hand round at the poky flatlet, the nondescript furniture.

"You'd taken my daughter away from me, hadn't you? I didn't need a whole house when there was only me."

"Oh, I don't think a woman like you loses the taste for a little bit of luxury—house and garden, nice furniture, nice clothes. All those things were part of the image. And they hid a very nasty reality, didn't they?"

"I don't know what you're talking about."

Oddie leaned forward.

"The reality being that you were running the show."

"There was no show."

"Oh, yes, there was. There was a ring, efficiently organized, discreetly run." He spoke confidently to mask his conviction that the whole business had been badly handled by the police officers concerned at the time. "There were something like twenty children regularly involved, and more drifting in all the time. And there were God knows how many clients—assured of anonymity, at a very high price. We never got to the bottom of who was running the show. As far as we were concerned, you were just a negligent mother. That was our mistake. Or did you manage to slip a hefty bribe to someone in the force?"

She had brought a shutter down over the face, all except that tight, mean little mouth. Now there was an unpleasant smile twitching the corners of it.

"Or was one of our people involved in the trade itself?"

The shutter stayed down.

"Anyway, what really interests me here and now is what're you doing at the moment?"

"Living my life and keeping myself to myself."

"I'm sure you're living your life. In fact, I think you're quietly going back to your old life, aren't you?"

"You know very well my daughter's in care. I'm only allowed to see her once a week, and then that bleeding woman she's with stands guard like she was a wardress in Holloway Prison. I've given up going—it's not worth the aggro."

"So you've severed all connection with your daughter? Funny, isn't it, that you've been seen coming back to the flat here with children."

A slight flicker crossed the eyes, the first sign that Oddie had seen of apprehension.

"I said children, not a child. One of your neighbors had seen you even before the night of the fire at the Phelans with a young girl. He wondered at the time whether you had a daughter living with you here. He's seen you since, also with a girl, but he's quite sure it was a different child. One was very fair, the other quite dark. He's also seen you with a young boy." Oddie thrust a big finger in her face. "It's obvious, isn't it? You're getting a ring together again."

"God! Can't I bloody *talk* to a child now?"

"Well, let's say you should be damned careful when you do. And this wasn't just talking: It was bringing them here to the flat, or taking them away again. I'm going to ask you to come along with us in a moment, but I've got one more question for you first. There was a child—girl or boy, I don't know—in this flat on the day the Phelans came with permission to view, wasn't there?"

Now there was a mulish expression on her face. Her business had been built on secrecy, on complete protection for the client. Even a scrubby little tart like June Phelan had had some idea of the importance of that. Mrs. Hobbs said nothing. Oddie went on:

"I don't suppose you were here yourself, were you? You procured the child, the client arrived, and you discreetly took yourself off. No doubt that's usual practice. Spares you any nastiness, doesn't it, and makes the client feel freer. But I want to know the name of your client that day."

She stared ahead, her narrow mouth pursed.

"If you keep quiet, you could find yourself accessory to a murder."

The impenetrability of a palace wall faced him. He leaned forward till their faces were close.

"I bet I could guess the name."

He spoke the name, and across her face there came a flicker that was incontrovertibly a spasm of fear.

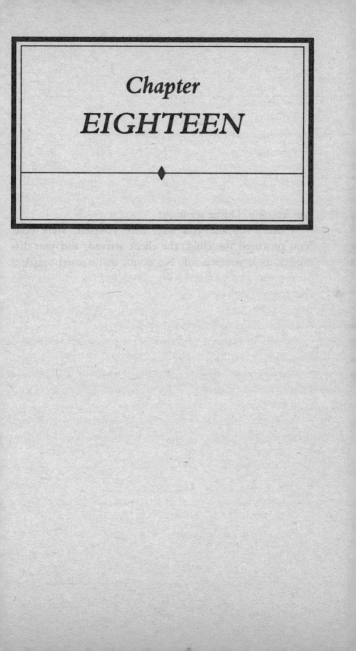

Chapter

EIGHTEEN

♦

---◆---

Stubborn as a mule," said Mike Oddie next day, after a second and a third attempt at denting the obdurate blankness of Mrs. Valerie Hobbs. "She's giving nothing, and she will give nothing."

They were in Oddie's office at police headquarters, looking down on the markets and arcades of Sleate and at the crowds scurrying to bus stops as rush hour began.

"She's aiming to go back into business," said Sergeant Stokes. "We can charge her, put her away for a bit, but she'll be starting up again, and round here too."

"That's right. Here's where her customers are. From her point of view there's no alternative to total noncooperation. Normally you might expect her to sacrifice somebody—name a name that doesn't matter to protect the ones who do. But in her game, her horrible game, it's absolute confidentiality that matters—the client's only protection. It's the code she lives by, her Masonic oath."

"She certainly wasn't giving anything away on the name that matters," observed Stokes gloomily.

"Of course not. The names with clout are central to her livelihood. It's there she's vulnerable, though."

"How did you come to hit on that particular name, sir, apart from the obvious thing?"

"I looked at everything we've learned since the fire, and everything that has happened over the last year or so that might have a connection with the case, and I noticed every little inconsistency, everything that didn't quite add up. In a case like this it's often a matter of registering little disquiets. Even so it was a guess, no more. How cooperative are the receptionists at the Burtle Group Practice—ever had anything to do with them?"

"Now and then. They're pretty good. They know Pickering has done a lot of work for us, so usually they'll come across with information—not confidential medical stuff, of course."

"Of course not."

"For anything other than routine they'd have to go to the doctor concerned, and, of course, he or she may often prove niggly. There are five or six medics in that group, and they're not all as cooperative as Pickering."

"Right. But what I'm after is hardly confidential medical stuff. What time is it? Just after five. I suppose the evening session starts at six, does it?"

"Yes, I think so. But I don't think tonight is one of Pickering's nights."

"No matter. I just want to talk to the girls in the outer office. I just might be able to confirm a hunch."

He raised his eyebrows at Stokes, and they smiled with the confidence of people who understood each other.

Steven Copperwhite did not feel like doing anything much about his move before Evie went out for the evening. He piled up some books against the wall of the study, got together a mass of papers, but beyond that it would have to wait. Really all he'd have to take would be a sort of symbolic essence of his presence in Wynton Lane. He was quite sure Evie would acquiesce good-humoredly in his move out, and let him come back any time he liked to remove more stuff. So it was just a question of clothes, typewriter, essential books, lecture notes.

At half past six, Evie poked her head around the door.

"Right. I'm off."

"OK. Where is it tonight?"

"Grantham."

"The Holy City! What are you doing there?"

"It's a symposium on strategies for women in the postfeminist age. With Doreen Appleby the MP."

"Hmmmm. She's nobody's favorite woman MP. On the other hand, who is?"

"Pig," said Evie cheerfully.

"Have a good time."

He heard her march down the hall in her usual swinging fashion, her clogs clattering on the parquet flooring. He could feel his heart beating fast: His life was turning another corner. When the front door banged, it had to his ears a ring of finality. He waited for the asthmatic wheeze of her car starting up and driving off, then he darted to the bedroom they had shared, opened the wardrobe wide and started collecting together his clothes.

He piled everything up in the hall. Books represented by far the largest share of what he felt he had to take. Steven's lectures were famous for the skill with which he juggled around other people's opinions. Lastly, when he had everything sorted out and ready, he went back into the study to write Evie a note. He had been working out the terms of it all day.

Darling Evie,

I feel it is time we admitted that you and me joining forces hasn't worked out. None of the blame for this is yours. You were totally honest, and laid down the terms before we started out. I am only sad I've failed to live up to you. I have loved your energy, your enthusiasms, your freshness. One day I know you'll find a man worthy of them. Can I hope that we shall always meet as friends?

Loving goodbye,
Steven

He wondered where to put it. The kitchen was the obvious place: Evie usually made herself a drink of hot chocolate when she came back late. But the mess of plates and packets and saucepans on the kitchen table and on all the other surfaces made that idea impracticable, and he was damned if he was going to wash up. In the end he shut the kitchen door and stuck the note onto it with sticky tape. Not very romantic, he thought, but it would have to do. It did not strike him that the end of a romance is not very romantic.

Before loading up the car he went up to one of the back bedrooms to see that there was no one around in the gardens. Not that there was likely to be on a dark November evening, but sometimes Lynn Packard worked on his car in the well-equipped stone garage he had had built. And Steven, though he was not at all ashamed of what he was doing, was distinctly embarrassed. No—all clear. No one around at all.

He went out, opened his garage, then opened the boot and the back doors of his car. Then he worked swiftly and efficiently. Back and forth he went, ten trips in all, and his life of the past three years was stored in his car. He shut the doors and went back into the house, congratulating himself on his efficiency, forgetting that he was efficient because he had done this before. He felt, faintly warming, a little wash of sentimentality. Really the only memories he cherished of his years here were centered on the bedroom. Still, this was the end of something—a chapter of his life, now closed. He took one last look around, then switched off all the house lights and went out to the car.

A light drizzle had started. He reversed the car out, turned it where the lane widened out, then drove round the curve that skirted Daphne Bridewell's house and out into Wynton Lane. He decided to drive through the Estate. Easier than going up to the Battersby Road. As he drove up the slope he had to swerve to avoid a rangy brown mongrel which was copulating with an Alsatian. He ran over a nasty patch of broken bottles and flattened a soft drink can. As he passed the blackened shell of the Phelans' home, he thought: Odd—all this fuss there's been about that man Phelan and I don't think I ever actually set eyes on him.

Five minutes later, driving toward the Horley district and his old home, the car began to hiccup oddly, not to respond to his driving intentions. Oh Lord, a flat, he thought. That glass on the bloody Belfield Grove Estate. Luckily there was a garage only minutes away, and he drove in and confirmed his fears. To his chagrin there was only a young girl in the office.

"I seem to have a flat tire," he said to her diffidently.

"Need any tools?"

"Well, actually, I'm not sure if I can change a wheel. I have done it once, but then I had someone with me to direct me. I don't suppose for a moment you—?"

"Sure. No problem."

And it wasn't. In hardly more than ten minutes the wheel was off, the spare on, the car ready for the road again. Really, young women these days were wonderful. In fact, almost frightening. In spite of living with Evie all that time, women capable in traditional men's spheres still made him feel awkward. Steven paid without a murmur the distinctly steep charges, and drove off.

The drizzle had ceased now, but light twinkled greasily on the damp road and pavements. There were few people around, and those that were were scurrying into pubs and off-licenses and fast-food places. Before long he was approaching Horley. Horley was the University part of Sleate, and somewhere he naturally felt at home. Somehow his residence in Burtle had never seemed real, not entirely serious. His old home, in a quiet street not far from the residential heart of Horley, seemed to him a place of great peace, security, stability. It would be good to be back there.

It was a quarter to nine when he drew up outside it. No lights on, but Margaret had told him she'd probably be working late. He could settle himself in, maybe prepare a bit of supper for her when she came back. He wondered what the old rooms looked like, what changes she had made. He wondered where he would be sleeping.

He got out and shut the car door quietly. All the houses around had lights on downstairs and curtains drawn. Good. He would be back and settled in before the tittle-tattle started. He opened the gate and saw that Margaret had left the porch light on. Considerate of her. The front garden seemed in good nick, though the buddleia could do with more cutting back. He slipped into the porch, took out his key, and put it into the lock.

Only it wouldn't go in. Odd. It was an ordinary Yale lock, and his old key, he felt sure. He jiggled it, but the lock resisted. He pushed it, trying to force it, then bent down to look closer. It was a new lock. So new as to be still bright and shining. Could Margaret have forgotten and—?

A dreadful realization washed over him. The lock was *brand* new. New since Margaret had handed him the key. She had played on him a cruel and humiliating jape. And suddenly, standing there, foolish, under the porch light another conviction invaded him: He was being watched. Someone was watching him now, and enjoying his plight. Not someone—two people. Women.

In the darkened bedroom of the house opposite—it was the house of the Fredericksons, whose cat Margaret was feeding while they were in Tunisia—she handed the opera glasses to Evie and wiped the tears of laughter from her eyes.

"I saw it," she said. "I saw him realize that he'd been tricked. And I saw something else, I swear: I saw him gripped by the conviction that he was being watched."

"He's going now," said Evie. "Scuttling away I'd call it, wouldn't you? . . . You know, I'm rather ashamed of enjoying this so much. I'm not a cruel person as a rule."

"I owe him one," said Margaret grimly.

"For his leaving you?"

"The *way* he left me. I'd gone to Peterborough to fetch my mother for a stay with us. I arrived back to find my husband gone, leaving the male equivalent of a 'Dear John' letter on the kitchen table. My marriage blown apart under the relentless gaze of my mother."

"I didn't know that."

"I wasn't accusing you of anything. . . . I wonder where he'll go now."

"Well, the lock on the back door of Ashdene should be changed by now. There's a nice man on the Estate who helps with the youth club—he was going down to change it as soon as the lights were off in the house. The front door bolts, so it doesn't matter. Do you think he'll go to one of the children?"

"No. The nearest is Susan—she lives at York. But he doesn't get on with her husband. Maybe a colleague—oh, no: Steven can't stand ridicule."

"That's true. Though he's quite good at jokes, isn't he? When I said I was going to Grantham tonight (actually it's tomorrow) he said: 'The Holy City!' Quite funny, I thought."

"He'll work it into one of his lectures soon. He's got a big repertoire of anti-Thatcher jokes. Do you know he said he was coming back to me because he needed rest? I nearly said I wasn't a Slumberdown mattress. Why do we always bite back remarks because we think we would regret them later, forgetting that we would thoroughly enjoy saying them at the time?"

"Women's conditioning. Still, this was better than a conversational put-down. . . . I suppose he'll go and stay in a hotel and start looking around for something to rent."

"At least I shan't get any calls from him in the future."

"Hardly. Do you think you'll marry again?"

"If somebody asks me." When Evie's expression showed the shock of the young and liberated, she explained, "Sorry. I meant if someone in particular were to ask me. What about you?"

"Never. I'm so glad to be rid of him, you've no idea! And so painlessly, thanks to you. Now I've escaped, I'll never try marriage again."

"Maybe it wasn't really marriage you tried."

"It was near enough!" said Evie feelingly.

◆

When Oddie and Stokes drew up in the little car park beside the handsome and substantial stone house that served the Burtle Group Practice it was eight o'clock and near the end of surgery time. They had been delayed because the duty sergeant had made the elementary error of putting a black youth in the same custody cell as Kevin Phelan. The delay had served its purpose, though, for there was by now only one receptionist on duty, and she was in a hurry to get home.

"I wonder if you could help me," said Oddie, showing his ID to the pleasant middle-aged woman when she slipped open the glass panel of the reception desk. "I know Dr. Pickering isn't on duty tonight, but it's a little matter concerning one of his patients—just a small matter, no question of confidentiality or anything."

"That's quite all right," said the woman, bustling away

to the filing cabinet. "I know Dr. Pickering is always happy to help the police. Who is it?"

"Kevin Phelan."

"Oh, *that* family," said the receptionist feelingly, bringing the file over and laying it on the desk top in front of the reception window. "What was it you wanted to know?"

"I want to know the date Kevin Phelan came to surgery here with burns on his hands. . . . Oh, and I had a question about Mr. Adrian Eastlake too."

The receptionist bustled away to the files again, leaving Kevin Phelan's file open. Oddie briskly cast his eyes down the upside-down entries. The woman soon came back with the second file, and opened it.

"I'd like to know when Adrian Eastlake last consulted Dr. Pickering for himself."

"Oh, that was a long time ago. March 1985. It's usually the mother, isn't it? . . . And Kevin Phelan seems to have consulted about burns in February this year—the twentieth."

"That's very kind of you—very helpful."

"Dr. Pickering's not on duty tonight, but he is in his consulting room if you want to have a word with him. He's catching up on some of the paper work."

Oddie took an instant decision.

"That might be useful."

"Just go through the archway there. His door is the first on the left. Just knock—but there's no one with him."

There was a firm "Come in" to their knock on the door. The doctor was writing when they went in, but he folded the paper and shook hands with both of them, ushering them to worn leather armchairs that had felt the backsides of thousands of Burtle's sick and malingering.

"Saw you arrive. Anything you wanted?"

"Well, your receptionist has helped me a bit. But there's something odd that I don't quite understand. It's about Kevin Phelan's visit to you—the time when he came with burns on his hands."

"Oh, yes. Actually it was Evans who saw him, I think."

"That was what was puzzling me. I saw the file on him in the office, and the entries—"

"Oh, you've just seen the office file." Pickering bustled up and started toward a filing cabinet in the corner of the consulting room. "That's just a duplicate. I keep the originals here, and I can show you—"

Mike Oddie could never really blame himself for his slowness. He could see only the man's back as he bent over the files, and it was only when he turned slightly back toward the light that he saw he had taken from within the files a pistol, and by then it was in his mouth. By the time he was out of his chair, the shot had rung out and Pickering was crumpling to the floor.

Later, when his colleagues on duty had pronounced him dead, and as Oddie and Stokes waited for the technical staff from headquarters to arrive, the flurry of photographers and measurers, the first official undertakers of the violently dead, Oddie went over to the desk and found the note on Pickering's blotter. It was barely legible, in doctor's scrawl, probably begun when he saw the men arrive in the car park outside.

Dear Oddie,

I wish I could explain how there came a time when fantasy was not enough, when I had to have the reality, and how, once I'd had it I needed it again—needed it so much, and so often. Better men, stronger men, would

have resisted, that I know, and I have nothing to plead
but

The note had broken off as the policemen had knocked
at his door.

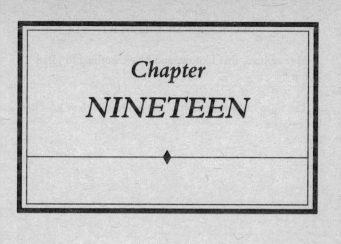

Chapter
NINETEEN

♦

---◆---

Algy?"

This is becoming a habit, Algy Cartwright thought.
Who would have imagined a few weeks ago that he and
Rosamund Eastlake would become linked on a near-
permanent chat-line? Still, it broke the day up pleasantly
enough.

"Yes, Rosamund."

"Algy, I'm going to ask you to do something for me.
Just refuse if it's inconvenient. I wondered if you would be
awfully kind and come up with me to the shops."

"Of course, Rosamund. Delighted that you feel you
want to. Or would you prefer me to drive you to the
shopping center?"

"No, Algy, not the shopping center yet. I don't think I
could cope yet with the trollies and the crowds. So just the

little local shops today. But perhaps in the future, if you were free . . . ?"

"Of course. Always happy to oblige."

"I have these plans—little plans—of taking things stage by stage. Eventually I want to go into Sleate, go shopping at Schreiber's again, though I know it will be sadly changed like everything else. Then before long I want to take in a matinee at the Palace, morning coffee somewhere pleasant . . ."

"Well, any time you want me to squire you, I'd be proud and happy to."

"Would you, Algy? I should be awfully grateful. It does take time to get confidence back, you know."

"I'm sure it does. Well, any time you want to do anything while Adrian is at work, you just give me a bell. . . . One thing, though, Rosamund: You don't think Adrian will resent my muscling in, do you?"

"Oh, Algy, the whole point is that I want to leave Adrian free to lead his own life at last—have friends, go to things, get out and about. All those years the poor boy has been waiting hand and foot on me—I want to make up to him for them. And really, Algy, I'll feel much happier with somebody of my own generation. So if you *were* willing . . ."

"More than willing, delighted. When shall we have our little expedition to the shops?"

"Well, the children have all gone to school, so there won't be too many people around. Say in twenty minutes?"

"I'll be round then."

As he put down the phone Algy Cartwright felt a surge of pleasurable anticipation jog through his veins. It was something, at his age, to have the prospect of squiring a good-looking woman around. That Rosamund Eastlake was still eye-catching he knew from the glimpses he had had of her in her garden in recent weeks. He thought: She's asked me rather than Daphne. Quite an honor, really. When it comes to the point women *do* feel a man is more of a protection. He foresaw many pleasant expeditions with Rosamund Eastlake under his wing. A moment's doubt whether she would consider him—well, *good* enough for matinees at the Palace or morning coffee quickly evaporated: After all, who else was there? And he would be doing a good turn to that poor-spirited son of hers too. It was wonderful how life was reacquiring an interest, a savor.

He went upstairs, opened his wardrobe, and on consideration changed into his good suit.

"Mum's coming out of hospital tomorrow," said Michael.

Mrs. Makepeace wasn't quite sure how to respond to that. "That will be nice" hardly corresponded to the facts of Phelan family life.

"Where will you be living?"

"They've put us in a house at the bottom of the hill—the Snowcroft Estate. It'll be nearer the school."

Mrs. Makepeace's heart sank a little. She enjoyed her visits from Michael, even if they often involved other young Phelans as well. There was a warmth and a joy about sitting with him, as now, in her kitchen, watching him eat, watching him stay normal, wholesome, and good-natured. It renewed her faith in life. She'd see less of him if he was down the hill, though the fact that he'd come to see her now, in his dinner hour, must mean he didn't want to throw off the connection.

"What about furniture?" Lottie asked. "There won't be much left from next door after the fire."

"There's a bit, but it smells *horrible*," said Michael, wrinkling up his nose. "The Social Security say they can't give us a grant for furniture, only a loan that we have to repay. But how's my Mum going to do that? I think it's daft. My Dad used to screw all sorts of special grants out of them and spend them down the Railway King, but my Mum can't get things that we need. Why?"

Because your Dad was a loud-mouthed bully and your Mum hasn't got what it takes, Lottie Makepeace felt like saying. Instead she suggested, "Maybe Malcolm Cray could help."

Michael nodded.

"He said he would try, but he says they're very strict these days. Malcolm and Selena have got some furniture they don't want in the new house. . . ." Michael toyed with the slice of fruit cake, fresh from the oven, that Lottie had pressed on him. "I don't think my Mum will be able to cope."

"Oh, she'll cope if she has to," said Lottie, with a brisk confidence she was far from feeling.

"I don't think she will. . . . If Kevin's in jail that'll help, and if June's not around much. But there's the little ones, and there's Cilla. . . . Did you know Dr. Pickering shot himself?"

"Yes, I knew."

"It was Cilla as caused all that. She's odd."

"She didn't cause it, you know, Michael. What caused it was going on long before Cilla took a hand. What about you? You'll be able to help your mother a bit, won't you?"

"I'll try. But I'm only twelve."

"Oh, nobody's asking you to take the world's problems

on your shoulders, young man! You could bring the two little ones up to see me now and again, though, couldn't you? Give your Mum a bit of a break."

"Yes, I'll do that. I'll still have you, won't I?"

"You will, Michael. Always welcome here."

"And Malcolm and Selena. They said I was to come back whenever I wanted, even when the baby's born."

There seemed to be about him an urge for self-protection, a feeling that the Phelan family's situation in the future might be still more hopeless than it had been in the past, a morass that might suck him down. She felt in him a consciousness that he was something different, that he might have something in himself that needed to be saved from corruption.

"And there's your teacher," she said, "that nice Miss Southgate. She's very interested in you.

"Yes, she is. And Mr. McEvoy. They say I should try for the school play. Dad wouldn't have let me, but I don't suppose Mum will bother."

"You'll be all right," said Lottie Makepeace. "You'll see: Somehow or other you'll come through."

◆

"Any chance of your taking an early lunch?"

Margaret Copperwhite turned and saw Mike Oddie leaning over her shoulder. His bulky geniality always made her smile with a warmth that Steven had never evoked.

"Oh, I think so. I'd have to ask the boss, but there's nothing pressing on at the moment."

"I've asked Malcolm Cray and his wife to meet me and Stokes in the Bowler's Arms at twelve-fifteen. They do one of the worst pub lunches in Sleate at the Bowler's, so we should be able to get a bit of privacy. I'm filling them in on the Phelan case—it was Cray saved the rest of the family, after all, and, of course, they're involved with Michael now. Thought you might like to come along, since your husband was involved too."

"Ex-husband."

"Seen him recently?"

"Seen. Not to talk to."

"That's all over, isn't it?"

"Super specially over."

"See you there at twelve-fifteen."

It has nothing to do with Steven, Margaret thought. He's involving me in his work. Life for Margaret, as for Algy Cartwright, seemed to be gaining a new savor.

Later, seated at a table at the Bowler's well away from the other early lunchtime eaters, with a plate of regrettable lasagne complete with chips and peas in front of her, Margaret suddenly thought: Is this going to be my life in the future—talking and socializing with policemen and their wives? She looked around at Malcolm and Selena Cray, at Sergeant Stokes and Mike Oddie. Compared with the academics she had been used to socializing with in the past, the new group would certainly be pleasanter, and probably more intelligent. Better-looking too.

I must not count my chickens, she told herself.

"It was a shock to us," Malcolm Cray was saying. "He was our doctor. I hadn't had much to do with him myself, but Selena'd been going to him all through the pregnancy."

"How did you find him?" Oddie asked her.

"Perfectly pleasant. Brisk, businesslike, maybe even a bit short, but that's not surprising in a G.P. these days." She thought for a moment. "Perhaps, looking back, there was something . . . somehow secretive about him. Some feeling that he was knotted up inside. But that's probably hindsight coming into it."

"His colleagues at the group practice say they felt they never really knew him," said Oddie. "But that's said of so many people, especially when they've committed suicide or got involved with a mucky case like this. The colleagues have always put it down to something in his personal life: He has a wife with a history of mental problems."

"Did his sexual orientation spring from her mental problems, or did her mental problems spring from his sexual orientation?" asked Margaret.

"Exactly," said Oddie approvingly. "The unanswerable chicken and egg conundrum. We'll never know. What is true is that she's coping surprisingly well with his death. Maybe it's a relief and a liberation."

"What put you on to him in the first place?" Malcolm asked.

Oddie's forehead crinkled.

"The first place—that's rather difficult to say. What made it clear we had to move him into the picture was the discovery that Mrs. Hobbs had a past and was connected with the Carrock business. Maybe if we'd looked at the houses in Wynton Lane a bit more thoroughly we'd have suspected something fishy earlier."

"Why?" asked Selena.

"Who lets the flat in his house just as he puts the house on the market? Even though Mrs. Hobbs told anyone who asked that it was just short-term, it obviously reduced its salability. Even these days it's notoriously difficult to unseat sitting tenants. If she'd had her daughter living with her, it could have been seen as a 'kind gesture.' But she hadn't. She was a perfectly capable woman on her own. That flat in the basement would be a very attractive 'plus' for anyone looking for a house with a granny flat, for example. Having the flat occupied—and with rather limited access, I imagine—made the house as a whole much less attractive commercially."

"Do you think she blackmailed him into letting her have it?" Selena asked.

"I doubt it. Mrs. Hobbs is very hot on the miserable ethics of her horrible trade. Blackmail involves a threat of exposure, and she kept her clients by an assurance of absolute secrecy. No—I think he let her have it because she promised him the sort of services he'd made use of in Carrock until two years ago. She was getting a ring together again."

"What did his note say?" remembered Sergeant Stokes. "Something about how once he'd had it he needed it again—like it was a drug, and the need kept increasing."

"That's it. I think he was asking for sympathy, though I can't find it in me to give him much."

"Do the flats in those houses connect with the main part of the house?" Margaret asked.

"Yes, they do. Staircase leading to a door. You see the convenience of it, don't you? He could go to the house in Wynton Lane any time he wanted to without arousing suspicion. He would merely be inspecting his property, making sure that there'd been no break-in, no squatters. He need never be seen actually going into the flat."

"You said—or implied—" said Malcolm, "that the Hobbs business wasn't the first time you wondered about Pickering."

"You told me you looked at everyone connected to the case and noted things that didn't add up," said Stokes. "I can think of things that didn't add up, but for the life of me I can't think of any that led back to Pickering."

"Little things," said Oddie, remembering. "Things not really remarked on at the time. Remember when we went to Kevin Phelan's flat, Stokes, and he tried to hide his burned hands? Just before he threw himself on me he said he'd been to Dr. Pickering with them. But when I rang Pickering to ask him about that he got the file on Phelan and said he had been to the surgery, but that he'd seen someone else."

"Either of them could have misremembered," commented Margaret.

"True. But just before I went along to the group practice I talked to Phelan, and in among the effing and blinding he insisted that he'd seen Pickering. When I saw his file I saw that all the entries were in the same hand. Pickering could have misremembered if I'd asked him cold, but not with the file in front of him. He had lied."

"But why?"

"Ah—" Mike Oddie stretched back in his seat and took a quick swig of bitter. "You see the problem is that we think of a premeditated murder as something brilliantly planned in advance by a cool mind, meticulously thought out, and so on. But this one wasn't like that. It was done by a man in a corner, a man thrashing around, not knowing what to do, uncertain how much was known about him, a man who committed murder because he didn't see what else he could do. . . . This steak and kidney pie is quite awful—all gravy. Are the other things awful too?"

"Quite disgusting," they all agreed.

"I obviously chose the right place," said Oddie with satisfaction, and looking around the dimly lit interior. "Almost deserted. A pub lunch has to be really rotten to get so few takers. Where was I? Right—with Kevin Phelan. There was another slight oddity here that struck me. Say Kevin Phelan *did* go to Dr. Pickering, as he insisted. Why didn't Pickering tip the wink to us at the time? The case of the burning-out of the Pakistani family was front-page news and there was general shock: The mother of the family and one of the children were killed. There really was a feeling of shame and revulsion. Pickering didn't have to break any oath and say 'Kevin Phelan came to me today with burned hands.' It could have been 'Wouldn't it be a good idea to have a look at young Phelan?' That's the sort of tip-off he'd given us in the past. Because the fact is Pickering was known for his helpfulness to the police— very much more helpful than some of his colleagues, I can tell you."

"Do you think that helpfulness was in itself suspicious?" Margaret asked.

"As a sort of advance insurance, in view of his activities? That may be so, though, of course, we never suspected anything of the sort. Anyway, he tipped us no wink about Kevin Phelan. And the reason, I'm sure, was that he already felt on uncertain ground in his dealings with the Phelan family."

There was a moment's silence.

"Because of June," Selena said.

"Exactly. Because both were involved with the Carrock business, one as child prostitute, one as customer. How specific his fears were I don't know. Whether he thought she'd seen him with one of the other children, whether he was afraid the girls talked among themselves, whether Mrs. Hobbs had made the ghastly mistake of introducing him to one of his own patients—there could be any number of reasons for his fear. June, the silly cow, is saying nothing, like Madam herself, so we can't know for certain. But I am sure that Pickering knew that June was for a time one of the ring—that was common knowledge around the Estate—and I'm sure he was afraid that June knew about him."

"So when Kevin came along," said Malcolm, "there was no question of shopping him, for fear of Phelan reprisals. And when you asked him, he was caught on the hop."

"That's right. Afraid we might say 'You could have given us a hint,' so—thrashing around, like I said—he lied and said yes, Kevin had been, but he'd seen someone else. But then, of course, he was in a desperate corner, because by then he *knew* one of the Phelan family was on to his activities, and he'd tried to wipe her out and had failed."

Malcolm Cray shivered.

"I remember we discussed this early on, and I assumed that whoever did it chose that night because he knew some members of the family would be away. I couldn't have got it more wrong, could I?"

"No. The member he planned to get wasn't there. But he—childless, and not living locally any longer—was not likely to know she would be away on a school theatre expedition. I think we could have been a bit sharper about Cilla as the intended victim from the start. We were blinded by the abundant awfulness of Jack Phelan. But we did register that Cilla had the little box room leading off from the hall as her bedroom. Right at the center of the fire. And who was likely to know she'd moved there, apart from her family and doubtless her best friend?"

"Her doctor," said Margaret.

"Michael told me Cilla had been off school recently," said Selena. "Bronchitis, I think he said."

"Right. Pickering knew where she slept. I think he wanted to get as many members of the family as possible—

281

that's what makes this case so shocking. I think the more he got the safer he would feel. But the prime target was Cilla."

"What exactly happened the day the Phelans went to The Hollies?" asked Margaret.

"There we have to guess, though we have one hard fact to go on. It's not possible to frighten Cilla into telling the truth now—if it ever was—by telling her she's at risk. She knows Pickering is dead, and she is both a secretive and a stupid child. What we can be quite sure happened is that she came well ahead of the main phalanx of Phelans, went up to the front door, then disappeared down the steps to the flat. After that is guesswork. Obviously the curtains must have been imperfectly drawn. I can't believe Pickering would have left lights on—though people sometimes behave incredibly stupidly in that sort of situation. She was gone some time, so I suspect she found the chink in the curtain, and peered until her eyes were accustomed to the gloom. That would have been in character. She knew exactly what was going on, of course. She was a Phelan. She recognized Pickering, and possibly recognized the child he was with—we don't know it would have been a little girl, by the way, but the wife said it would. What we do know is that he was telephoned at home two days later by a child."

"Cilla?"

"Almost certainly. The wife took it, the child was very insistent she speak to the doctor himself. After he'd taken it Pickering was very upset, though he tried to hide it. He said it had been one of his patients whose mother was ill, but his wife said he'd said very little to the child, and didn't go out to anyone afterward."

"It was then he conceived the plan?"

"Yes. By then he was already aware of the furor in Wynton Lane about the prospect of the Phelans moving in. He knew no more about the size of the pools win than anybody else. At first he may have thought that this was ideal—that it provided a plethora of suspects. But a moment's consideration must have told him that it could be fatal: Police interest in Wynton Lane could embrace Mrs. Hobbs, and then questions might be asked about why he'd let her have the flat, what connection there was between them. He could have shifted her out hurriedly, but that in itself would have aroused suspicion. The safest way was to make the killing as un-Wynton Lane as it possibly could be."

"Everyone seemed to want to suggest it was a working-class way of killing," said Sergeant Stokes.

"That's right. Bloody nonsense, of course! It really got my goat! The most you could say was that it was a National Front horror tactic, and most of the Front activists tend to be working class. Quite apart from the fact that this could have been a ploy to make us look anywhere but the correct direction. No, as I say, that riled me, and when I thought about it, thought back to the early days after the fire, it wasn't just the Wynton Lane people who jumped in with that suggestion: One of the first who'd taken that line had been Pickering. He'd been as quick to suggest it was a working-class crime as Kevin Phelan had been to accuse the people in Wynton Lane."

"In other words, it was all a rather desperate improvisation," suggested Margaret.

"Yes. Looking back at the talk I had with him the day after the fire I could trace the improvisation. First he clung to the possibility—he must have realized how remote that was—that the fire might be accepted as accidental. He didn't mention the Wynton Lane angle until I brought it up, then he gave me a full account of what he knew I could find out for myself. Then when I told him it seemed to have been deliberate he immediately latched on to 'Paki-bashing' and the working-class crime nonsense. I remember thinking at the time it was a pretty unintelligent line for someone of his experience to take. Thrashing around, you see."

"Do you think he realized how desperate his position was?" asked Malcolm.

"Yes. The gun in the filing cabinet shows that he knew the thing was poised on a knife edge. His strength was that we had no reason to connect him with the anti-Phelan campaign in Wynton Lane: He'd moved away, and he'd been notably unsympathetic when canvassed. His weakness was that if we got wise to who Valerie Hobbs was, we were going to start asking questions about how she came to be there."

"He had seen patients the morning he died," contributed Selena. "He may have heard gossip from one of them about Mrs. Hobbs being taken for questioning."

"Yes, he may have. There's not much has happened in Wynton Lane or on the Belfield Grove Estate over the last few weeks that hasn't been observed and commented on. If he heard, he could have been almost sure his number was up. But, in any case, I would guess that revolver had been there at least since the murder. Pickering was an intelligent man. He knew he was doing a makeshift job to avoid exposure and ruin, not a well-planned one. He must have realized that in the long run the odds were stacked against him."

"I know a policeman shouldn't say this," said Malcolm Cray, emptying his glass, "but I can't find it in me to regret that he managed to kill himself. His life in jail would have been unspeakable. I found I couldn't regret Phelan's death, and I'm afraid I can't regret Pickering's either."

"I'm inclined to agree," said Oddie. "And the fact is, we have two very satisfying cases coming up. With information we got from Waley we should be able to put Mrs. Hobbs away for a time, and we'll keep a very close eye on her once she comes out. And Jason Mattingley has been well-advised in Apsely Jail and has spilled the beans very comprehensively on Kevin Phelan, as I suspected he would. The problem with choosing someone very bullyable as your sidekick is that when the other side gets hold of him they can bully him too. We'll have young Kevin on charges of murder, extortion by intimidation, and much else besides. He'll be away for years."

Oddie looked at his watch.

"Heavens, is that the time? I'd best be getting back." He put his hand on Margaret's shoulder. "Come on. I'll walk you back to the station."

But it was not to be yet. As she got up, Margaret looked toward Selena Cray and saw that she had suddenly clutched the edge of the table and was looking up at her husband.

"Malcolm—don't panic, but I think it's starting. Could you get me to the Infirmary?"

So it was half an hour later, after Selena had been admitted, and after Malcolm and she had been waved off to the labor ward, that Margaret and Oddie started to walk back toward police headquarters.

"Nice to be in at the beginning of something," said Margaret.

"Yes," said Mike Oddie, and took her arm.

That afternoon Carol Southgate and Bob McEvoy had a date to go back to Bob's flat. Bob said he had had enough of braving the evil eye of Daphne Bridewell, but both of them knew he meant that he did not wish to go to bed with Carol for the first time with the evil eye of Daphne Bridewell hovering in the upstairs regions. Carol, in fact, heartily agreed. They began the walk still talking over the events of their day, really thinking about something else altogether.

"Miss Southgate! Mr. McEvoy!"

They turned and saw Michael Phelan darting out of the school gates, anorak half on and half off, and hair disheveled in properly schoolboy fashion.

"Mr. McEvoy, when did you say the auditions were for the school play?"

"December the first. The day after Speech Day."

"Right. Do you think I'll be all right at Speech Day?"

"You'll be fine. If you don't get nerves."

"I don't *think* I'll get nerves."

"And there are auditions in January for *Saint Joan*. That'll be for all the schools in Sleate, but there's a jolly good part for a younger boy."

"Well, I'll try for that too."

"No problems at home now?"

"Well, not about that. I'll just tell my Mum. My Dad would have kicked up a fuss, but I don't suppose my Mum will be interested."

"Isn't she out of hospital today?" Carol asked.

"That's right. That's our new home, over there." He

286

pointed to the Snowcroft Estate, where brick houses identical to those on the Belfield Grove Estate stretched out from the main road. "We'll be practically sleeping on the floor, and eating off it too, but I suppose we'll manage. I'd best go home now and see what's she's been doing." He grinned with a touch of self-derision. "I suppose you realize I'm the man of the household now? How about that!"

He raised his arm in farewell and ran off. They stood watching as he kicked a can along the gutter, weaved his way through traffic across the road, looked back at them in a frankly salacious way to see if they were holding hands, then danced off into the Snowcroft Estate, through the cans and the chocolate wrappings and the pizza cartons, dodging the strays and crunching on broken glass, touched by God's grace or explained by the theories of educationalists, racing forward to a future of normality, decency, and niceness almost beyond human comprehension.

They watched him till he was out of sight. Then they turned and resumed their walk up the hill.